CRUEL DEVIL

BY DANIELA ROMERO

Contents

About the Book

Dominique Price.
Good looking.
Arrogant.
Football-God and my brother's best friend.

He hates me.
He wants me.
He can never have me.

Everything comes so easy for him.

I refuse to be just another game for him to win.

Kasey

This year will make me or break me. Personally, I'm hoping for the former. But, as I sit in the back seat of my mother's SUV, I have a feeling it's going to be the latter. There's this sense of foreboding thrumming through me as I look up at the impeccably manicured lawns and twin pillars that decorate where I'll be living this next school year. All one hundred and eighty days of it, plus winter and spring breaks. I'm going to hate every minute.

I'm very much aware that there isn't a seventeen-year-old out there who wouldn't kill to leave the nest a little bit early. And trust me when I say I'm not feeling like my life is about to take a turn for the worse just because I'm moving out at the ripe old age of seventeen. What does have me feeling this way is the fact that I'm joining a sorority. Not by choice, I might add.

Sorority life isn't my scene. And no, I don't have any firsthand experience with sororities, and yes, I'm absolutely judging them based on what I've seen on TV, but let's be real, if you knew anything about me, you'd agree that me and the perfect plastics I see walking in and out of the houses on sorority row aren't a match made in heaven.

When I applied for Sun Valley High's running start program —a program that allows me to attend college courses and earn both college credits and the final credits I'll need for my high school diploma, I thought, *this is exactly what I need.* An escape from the stupid drama that is high school life where I never really fit in. It's hard to relate to the people at school when all they can talk about is how Suzie made out with Jason behind Ruby's back and other stupid nonsense, like who is asking who to senior prom.

Meanwhile, my best friends have all graduated and are planning their weddings and being moms and doing real-life things that matter. It makes it hard to relate to high-school life. Hearing the gossip and then seeing all the back-stabby antics, it's not what I'm interested in. And don't even get me started on the boys.

They're so incredibly stupid in high school. The catcalling and fuck-boy flirting. Urgh. You'd think they'd find a better pickup line than, "You must be an angel, because you look like you just fell from heaven."

Barf.

The guys I go to school with have zero game. Not that I'd be interested in anyone at Sun Valley High anyway. I almost wish I was. It'd make seeing a certain broody asshole on the regular a hell of a lot easier.

Both of us attending Suncrest U isn't going to help, but with any luck I won't see him any more than I have to. Suncrest University is his turf, and here he reigns supreme, not that I'm surprised. Dominique Price and his best friends ran the halls at Sun Valley High as the school's football gods, so of course their reputations would follow them to college as they continue to dominate on and off the field. I used to hate those three for what they put my brother through, but now we're all friends. Hell, more like family. But I don't need people realizing we know each other, especially with the unwanted attention that will bring, so I'd like to keep our association under wraps.

And since I'm in college now, Mom decided it was the perfect time to accept an out-of-state promotion and force me to join Kappa Mu—her alma mater. Guess that makes me a legacy.

Yay.

Not.

The alternative was moving with her—so not happening. The prospect of uprooting my entire life to move halfway across the country holds zero appeal, even if the alternative is, well, this.

"Ready to braid hair and paint your nails bubblegum pink?" my brother—Aaron—asks from the front seat.

I roll my eyes and flip him the bird. "Ha. Ha. You're so funny."

He turns to glance at me, pushing the blond hair from his face to give me a wink. "Don't worry, sis. They'll leave you alone once they realize what a prickly personality you have."

I lunge forward to smack him but he swings open the passenger side door, stepping out, just in time to avoid my swipe.

"Kasey!" my mother admonishes me.

"What? He started it," I tell her as I unbuckle to follow him. Despite the early hour, the house is already buzzing with activity—what looks to be a party in full swing. Girls in all manner of summer wear are flitting about, socializing, drinking whatever is in those red Solo cups—and let's be honest, it's not water—and carrying boxes, doing exactly what I'm here to do. Move in.

I wrinkle my nose and glance at my mom as she slings her oversized purse over her shoulder and moves to join Aaron and me on the sidewalk. "Not too late to change your mind?" Aaron mutters under his breath. "You know you wanna."

I elbow him in the ribs. "Are we telling jokes now?"

When mom concocted this grand idea of me joining her former sorority, Aaron, being the protective big brother he is, was nice enough to offer me the spare room at his place. An offer I was quick to decline.

Under normal circumstances, I'd consider it. We were never very close growing up given the four-year age gap between us, but Aaron has always looked out for me. Most brothers would balk at the idea of living with their baby sister after they moved out, but Aaron genuinely wouldn't mind. He's pretty chill about stuff like that.

The problem isn't living with my brother. It's living with my brother's very hot, very broody, drives-me-insane, asshole of a roommate—Dominique Price. On the best of days, we tolerate one another. On the worst, well, things can be openly hostile.

"I'll pass on living with the devil and take door number two, please," I tell him, and he chuckles.

"Dom isn't that bad."

I snort. "Are we talking about the same person, here?" Dominique Price very much is that bad. He gets under my skin in a way no one else can, and the pull he has over me, urgh. I hate it. Sometimes so much so that I think I hate *him*. When we're in the same room, I want to kiss him and punch him in the same breath. That he makes me question my own sanity is infuriating.

Aaron gives me a light-hearted shove. "Alright, sis, have it your way. But don't come crying to me when you realize the grass isn't greener on the other side."

A gust of wind blows my hair into my face and I hastily push my blond curls out of my eyes. "I won't," I assure him. "The grass on your side is already dead and yellow so the bar is set pretty low."

He smiles, his eyes scanning past me, and I turn to see a familiar black Escalade roll up beside my mother's car. The broody asshole I just mentioned parks his overpriced SUV and three doors open, letting out Dom, Roman, and Emilio. Somebody please shoot me now.

"What are they doing here?" I groan.

Aaron throws his arm over my shoulder and pulls me into a side embrace. "They're being good friends and helping you move into your new place." The fact that he genuinely believes that should be concerning, but I know better.

"Whose idea was this?" I ask.

Already their presence is drawing curious looks from some of the girls. It won't take long for them to realize who they are. God dammit, he is such an asshole. It would have been bad enough if he came on his own, but bringing Roman and Emilio is taking it one step too far.

"Dom's," Aaron confirms what I suspected and my mother being the weirdo she is, gushes.

"Isn't that so sweet of them, Kasey? It makes me so happy to know you'll have such a great support system here. Makes me feel so much better about my baby girl going to college." She sighs, the smile on her face wistful as she turns back to the house. If I grind my teeth any harder I'm liable to break a tooth. She cannot be serious right now.

"Yep. Soooo sweet," I tell her while giving Dominique my most murderous glare. Does he shake in fear like he should? Of course not. Instead he smirks like the cruel bastard he is and heads right for me, Roman and Emilio right on his heels.

I'm going to make him regret this. I cannot believe he'd set me up like this.

The guys do that guy handshake bro hug thing as if they didn't all see each other a few hours ago, then Dom turns his full attention on me and I have to force my expression to remain impassive. Age has only worked to sharpen his features, making him even more striking than the boy I met my freshman year of high school three years ago. With his hair tightly braided away from his face, his sharp jawline and full lips stand out in stark relief, and I can't decide if I want to kiss him or punch him—a frequent struggle of mine, so I do what I'm best at and just antagonize him.

"Are you so desperate for female attention that you have to drop in on the girls of Kappa Mu for a little bit of an ego stroke?" I smile in satisfaction when his dark brown eyes narrow.

Dominique has this edge to him that's difficult to describe. He's both regal and rugged; the juxtaposition between the two is likely what makes women flock to him. He has two thin slashes in his right brow that somehow take him from attractive to dangerous, and after graduation he filled out to a full six-foot-five, stacked with all the muscles you'd expect a division one athlete to have. The effect he has on people is hard to miss.

When he scowls the way he is doing right now, he's damn near terrifying to behold. But when he smiles, a real smile that doesn't hold an ounce of malice—and mind you those are rare—his entire face lights up and for a second it's like standing in the sun after months of nothing but rain. God, I hate him.

"I don't need an ego stroke. Not a single woman here can hold my interest," he says, his eyes boring into mine and waiting for a reaction. One I refuse to deliver. *Asshole.* Of course he'd say something like that. Dominique hasn't dated, like seriously dated, for as long as I've known him. He gets around, I'm sure. What football player doesn't when you have an entire fan club of jersey chasers? But the only girl I've seen him with more than once is Tamara Vinzent. I haven't had the pleasure of meeting her yet, but she's his date to any event or function that requires one. I don't really understand their relationship, and for my own sanity, I try not to think about it too much, but somehow she's outlasted everyone else and has managed to sink some form of a hold into Dominique where no others before her have succeeded.

When Dominique realizes I'm not going to respond, the corner of his mouth curls into his signature cruel smile. "You worried someone will catch my attention?" He scans the growing crowd. "Not really my type, but maybe I can—"

"Yo, Baby Henderson," Emilio says, cutting Dominique off from whatever he was about to say and cutting through the growing tension in the air. "You gonna show us the new digs? Introduce us to your new lady friends?" He winks, and if I didn't know him better, I'd think he was serious. But Emilio is head over heels in love with his girlfriend, one of my best friends, so I know this is for show and he's just helping me out. The softy. Too bad his little act of kindness won't keep him safe if he and the others don't get the hell out of here before anyone realizes the school's star quarterback, wide receiver, and cornerback just showed up.

I shake my head. "Hard no. You three need to leave."

Roman smirks and Emilio clutches his heart as though I just wounded him. "Baby Hen—"

"Stop calling me that and go home or I'm going to tell Bibi about your big surprise," I warn.

He sucks in a sharp breath. "You wouldn't. You love me?" He meant it as a statement but it comes out more as a question.

"Wanna bet?" Because today is day one of campus life for me and I'm not going to let these three muck it up.

Emilio backs away, hands raised in the air. "You win. I'll stay in the car." He turns and jogs back to Dom's Escalade. One down. Two more to go.

I turn to Roman and raise a single brow. "You too, mister."

"You don't have anything you can use against me," he says, his voice filled with confidence he should not be feeling right now. Doesn't he know me? I have something on virtually everyone. It's little sister 101. You always find the dirt and horde it to later get your way.

I prop one hand on my hip. "I don't?" I press a finger to my lips as though thinking before letting a wide smile spread across my face. "Hey, Aaron, did I ever tell you about the time Roman and Allie went to Silverdale?"

Roman's eyes widen briefly before his brows draw together. "How do you—"

I pull my phone from my back pocket. "Allie sent me pictures from that weekend. You two were so cute together. The couples—"

Roman jerks forward, pressing his palm over my mouth. His dark brown eyes fill with a mix of disbelief and fury. "Not. Another. Word," he growls. If he were anybody else, I might be worried by the threat in his voice, but despite his rough exterior, Roman is a big ole softie and his fiancé is one of my other best friends. He wouldn't hurt a hair on my head. She loves me. He loves her. Therefore, I win. So instead of pushing his hand away or trying to say anything, I wait for him to realize what I already know.

It takes only a handful of seconds.

"Fine. Don't say anything else. I'll go chill with E. Deal?"

I nod and he slowly releases me, hesitating for just a second to make sure I'll keep my mouth shut before he turns, slaps Dom on the shoulder with a muttered, "You're on your own, man," and joins Emilio in the car.

"Damn, sis, remind me not to get on your bad side," Aaron says, as if I haven't used this exact same tactic on him before.

"Got anything on this one?" He nods toward Dominique, who raises a brow of his own, expression smug because, no, I have nothing I can use against him to make him do anything he doesn't want to do and he knows it.

God, I hate him sometimes.

2

Dominique

I smile, watching the gears turn in that pretty little head of hers as she struggles to find a way to get rid of me. Not happening, baby girl. Kasey coming to Suncrest U is a disaster waiting to happen. She's seventeen for chrissakes, and her idiot mother thought it'd be a great idea for her to join the biggest sorority on campus. What a joke.

Football and training for football are what I'm focused on, so it's become a habit of mine to avoid all things Greek, but only a hermit wouldn't know Kappa Mu and their frat counterpart Alpha Ze are the two most notorious party houses here. Problem is, when shit goes down, it gets ugly.

There have been plenty of rumors about girls getting drugged and guys taking turns at some of their parties, and I'll be damned if anyone is going to try shit like that with Kasey.

I can't stand the girl, but that doesn't mean I'll sit back and let anything happen to her, either. I'm not a complete asshole, despite what she might think.

It's why I suggested to Aaron that she move in with us. I'm willing to take one for the team if I have to, not that it'd be some big hardship. I'm barely home during the week. Most of my time is spent in class, on the field, or at the gym, and most Saturdays I have games. Half of them are out of town.

I'm home on Sunday afternoons but usually gone in the evening to see my sister. Sundays are the obligatory Price family dinners. My parents made them mandatory when Monique and I moved out for college, and while I managed to find a way out of them, my sister wasn't so lucky. She goes to school out of state and she still has to fly in for those fucking dinners, so I make it a point to at least catch up with her while she's here and take her to the airport for her return flight whenever I can.

Where Kasey and Aaron's parents are damn near absent, mine take overbearing to an entirely different level.

Aaron liked the idea of Kasey moving in. He's protective of his little sister the same way I am of mine, so it should have been a done deal, except Kasey refused to get on board with the program. The pretty little idiot.

When she shot down the idea, there wasn't shit I could do about it, and Aaron wasn't willing to pressure her. Something about her being independent and responsible and yeah, compared to most females her age, maybe she is. But she's still young. Impressionable. Guys are going to take one look at her small body, perfect tits, and seductive mouth and think she's theirs for the taking.

"Why are you here?" she asks like she doesn't already know.

"I'm helping. That's what *friends* do." I put more emphasis on the word friend than necessary, but sometimes I need to remind myself that's what we're supposed to be. Friends. Not enemies. Not rivals. She's part of our crew, which means I'm obligated to look out for her same as I would for Allie and Bibiana—Roman and Emilio's girls.

But fuck, the way she gets under my skin, sometimes it's all I can do not to spank her ass to get her to behave. Kasey Henderson is a match just waiting to be lit, and I'm the spark that gets her temper roaring. The way we verbally spar with one another, her tongue like a whip intent on tearing me down, it makes my cock jerk just thinking about how she'd be in the sack. Would she be just as wild and unrestrained? Or would she be shy and submissive?

Get your shit together, D. I fight the urge to adjust myself and force my face to remain impassive. I'm not interested. Not really. I'm just also not blind. Kasey's all grown up. Her waist dips beneath her ribs, giving her an hourglass figure that should be illegal on a seventeen-year-old girl. Her tits are full and round and her ass is more than a handful that I've definitely considered squeezing a time or two. Again, not because I'm interested.

I lock down thoughts like that as soon as they occur. Kasey Henderson is one hundred percent off limits. For one, she is too fucking young. Four years might not seem like a big deal to everyone else, but it sure as shit is when the girl in question is a minor. And for two, I don't do relationships.

Between school and football, I don't have time for one, nor am I particularly fond of having someone all up in my business. Women are needy and temperamental. If the urge arises, I'll find a girl to take home for the night, but that's all I'm interested in. One night.

Besides, I'm pretty sure Aaron would have my balls if I made a play for her. There's an unspoken rule between friends. Thou shall not fuck one another's siblings.

He and I are damn near brothers at this point. No way can I cross that line.

After graduation, the plan was for Roman, Emilio, and I to get a place off campus together. But both fuckers had to go and couple up senior year of high school, so that plan went down the drain real quick and left me with two options. Move into the dorms—not fucking likely—or get my own place off campus. But then money would be tight and I didn't want to ask my parents to cover it. Doing that would lead to trouble. Nothing given was ever given freely, and I didn't want the strings I knew would be attached.

My grandmother set up a trust fund for my sister and I that we got access to the day we turned eighteen. It's not much, but it covers my monthly expenses and would cover rent on a house off campus if I could find a roommate.

The idea of living with a stranger isn't something I could get on board with, so I buried my shit with Aaron and got a place with him since the fucker was the only other one in our crew riding solo like myself.

Since he and the girls are all close, it made sense. We weren't going to be getting rid of him anytime soon. Looking back, it was the right call, even if I didn't love the idea at the time.

Aaron's good people. He fucked up when we were all kids but since then, when any of us need him, he shows up. He's there when it counts, and he's put his ass on the line for me more times than I can count. I won't repay that by banging his sister behind his back, even if there was that one time we kissed, and it still fucking haunts me.

"You good, man?" Roman asks.

I grunt, refusing to take my eyes off the girl in front of me. "Fucking peachy."

Roman snorts and places his hand on my shoulder.

"Right. Well, while you pine over baby Henderson, I'm gonna go get my girl before Emilio tries to steal her."

"I'm not pining," I retort. I don't pine after chicks, least of all a freshman with too much sass and too little sense. What the fuck does she think she's doing right now? And where the hell is her brother. Shouldn't he be watching her or something? At the very least, he should be fending off the assholes who just

want to take advantage of her. No way would I let guys be all over my sister like that.

He laughs, shaking his head. "Call it whatever you want but your jealousy is showing, man. Might want to get that in check."

I grind my teeth together, flipping off his retreating back. Rome doesn't know what he's talking about. Baby Henderson isn't anything special. A piece of ass and soon to be jailbait. Not someone I'd be jealous over.

Speaking of Hendersons, Aaron walks up beside me and hands me a Coke. I accept the drink, knowing the fucker is just being nice, and against my better judgement I ask, "You cool with older guys all over your baby sister?" I feign indifference and take a drink of the soda waiting to see how he reacts. It has nothing to do with wondering if the age difference between her and I would matter to him and everything to do with making sure he knows what's going on with Kasey right now.

As expected, Aaron follows my gaze. His eyes narrow and he mutters a curse. "Shit. I'll have to drag her away from a fucking harem and I'll have to deal with her bitching about it the entire way home today."

I force a laugh. "She's a handful."

He shakes his head. "That's putting it mildly. I don't know what her deal is, man. Lately, it's like she's looking for trouble." He sighs. "I better go deal with that."

I thrust a hand out to stop him. "Let me." I don't know why I made the suggestion but I don't try to walk it back once it's out there.

His dark blond brows pull together. "You sure, man?"

I nod. "Yeah. Let her be pissed at me. Then on the way home when she's bitching you can pretend to agree with what an asshole I am."

He smiles and slaps me on the back. "Thanks, man. I owe you one." I nod like it's no big deal. Just helping the guy out. I don't have a single selfish reason for making the suggestion.

Allie calls his name and Aaron turns. "Go," I tell him. "I'll get it handled."

He hesitates for a moment. "You sure, man? Kasey can be—"

I cut him off. "Bro, I've got it. Go see what Allie wants." He walks away, heading toward Roman and Allie on the other side of the yard, and without missing a beat, I head straight toward my quarry. She's got herself surrounded by some of Allie's friends from back home. I met the guys earlier, Gabe, Felix, and Julio. They seem nice enough, but that doesn't mean any of them should be talking to her right now.

When I'm within hearing distance I slow my steps, casually walking closer to the group. Gabe, who's on her right, is laying it on thick. He's smiling at her like she's all that he sees. Not happening, asshole.

As soon as I'm behind her, I pull her back into my chest and wrap my arms around her, pinning her in place with her back to my front. I ignore the way she feels pressed up against me and focus on the miscreants in front of me.

Kasey doesn't bother trying to twist to see who's grabbed her. My dark arms banded around her is telling enough. I'm the only black guy here. She doesn't have to see my face to know it's me, and being the smart girl she is, she doesn't bother putting up a fight to get away.

"You know Baby Henderson is jailbait, right?" I direct the question first to Gabe before making eye contact with the other two. Kasey stiffens in my arms and a beautiful shade of pink creeps up her neck.

"For you, maybe," Gabe retorts with a shrug.

The corner of Julio's mouth lifts into a smirk like he's in on some secret, but he doesn't say anything. He takes a drink of his soda and rocks back on his heels, watching things play out. Felix, on the other hand, gives a hard shake of his head. "Ain't no one trying to tap that," he says. "We're all friends. Just having a conversation. No one's crossing any lines."

Gabe snorts. "Speak for yourself," he tells him, and then looks Kasey right in the eyes. "I have no problem saying I am very much interested." He licks his lips and gives her a heated look that makes me want to punch the fucker in the face. "Wanna blow this place? Go have some fun?"

I can't see her expression, but if I had to guess she's probably eating this shit up, if only to irritate me more. "Why not?"

"She's fourteen," I grind out.

"I'm seventeen. Age is just a number, man." He shrugs.

Kasey squirms in my arms in an attempt to get away, but I shift her around, putting her firmly behind me before stepping up and getting in Gabe's face. "She's too young for you, so knock that shit off. No guy here is going to let you put the moves on Henderson's little sister."

Despite having to look up to meet my stare, Gabe doesn't back down. "Did it sound like I was asking for permission?"

Before I do anything that will land me on Allie's shit list, like beating her friend to a pulp, I turn on my heel and grab Kasey by the arm, pulling her with me as I go.

"Dominique, let go of me," she complains, but her steps follow. A glance over my shoulder shows Julio with a hand against Gabe's chest while he mutters something in his ear. Whatever it is, it keeps him in place and that's good enough for me.

I drag Kasey around the side of the house where no one can see us and press her up against the brick exterior, my arms caging her in on either side and offering her zero chance of escape.

Does she look worried? Not one fucking bit. The girl looks pissed and ready to raise hell.

"What is your problem! You had no right—" she snarls, shoving against my chest, but it's like a kitten swatting at a bull. I barely feel it. "You can't manhandle me like that. You are not my keeper. And you do not get to dictate who I hang out with."

"I have every right," I grind out the words and her eyes widen. Shit. I didn't mean for that to come out. The girl gets in my head. Under my skin. She is so goddamn infuriating.

"What is it exactly that gives you the—"

No answer is a good answer, so instead, I close the distance between us and capture her lips with my own to shut her up. At least that's what I tell myself. She jumps, but I don't let that deter me. I step forward into her space, pressing my mouth more firmly against her own and deepening the kiss while grabbing her beneath her thighs and lifting her into my arms. Her legs wrap around my waist instinctively and I press her back against the house. A small moan passes across her lips and I want to hear it again, so I press my hardening cock against her jean-clad center and grind my hips against hers.

She gasps, tearing her mouth away and sucking in a lungful of air. I nip at her full lips and trail kisses down her jawline. Her neck. All while thrusting my hips against her, letting her feel how badly I want her right now.

"What are you doing?" she asks with jagged breath.

I don't answer. Instead, I capture her lips again and drink down her soft sighs and sweet moans. If I were being honest with her, I'd say I had no fucking clue what I was doing, but as soon as I open my mouth to speak, all of this stops and I'm not ready for that to happen just yet.

I shake out the memories from that day and focus back on the here and now.

"We're not friends," Kasey retorts, arms folded across her chest and mouth pressed into a tight line.

I shrug like her words don't affect me.

"We're not even friendly," she adds.

She's not wrong. Since that kiss, shit between us has gone from bad to worse. Kasey and I are like cats and dogs, or oil and water. We don't mix. When we do, things get heated and not in a good way. It's my fault for the way things are between us, and I'm man enough to own that, but when I pressed my mouth against hers and swallowed her soft cries of pleasure I knew right away it was a mistake.

"I'm friends with him." I nod in Aaron's direction. "And I'd be a shit friend if I didn't at least offer to help the guy out. We both know he'll do most of the heavy lifting while you and your mom talk with whoever it is running this show."

Her jaw works and I can tell she's barely keeping herself in check. I love it when she gets like this. All fire and brimstone, ready to raise hell to get what she wants. But before she can say anything else, her mom tugs on her arm. "Kasey, leave the poor boy alone. He's only trying to help. Besides, there are so many things I want to show you before I have to leave." She tugs on her daughter's arm, who reluctantly follows, throwing one last look my way before admitting defeat.

I give her a small wave and her eyes narrow even further. She'll come up with a way to get me back.

I'm looking forward to it.

3

Kasey

I hate him. I hate him. I hate him. I repeat the mantra a dozen times in my head until I convince myself it's the truth. Why does he have to be so infuriating all of the time?

Mom doesn't give me long to dwell on it before she marches me right through the front doors and to the left down a long hallway. We pass a living room, dining room, and kitchen before coming to the open door of an office with a small gold placard that reads, "House Mother."

"Knock, knock," my mother calls before stepping inside, pulling me right along with her.

An attractive brunette looks up and greets us, a wide smile on her face. "You must be Mrs. Henderson?" she says, coming around her desk and shaking mom's hand.

"Ms. Douglas, actually. Kasey's father and I divorced years ago." She throws this out with a laugh like it's no big deal, but

I know mom hates it. Dad forced her to change her name after the divorce. Said she didn't deserve it and the perks that came with being a Henderson. He's an asshole and whatever perks come with my name I'm still waiting on to be delivered, but he's also my dad, so I'm duty bound to love him. Even when he's absent and downright cruel where mom is concerned. "But please, call me Helen."

"Nice to meet you, Helen. I'm Hilary, the Kappa Mu president," she says this with a sugary sweet smile so wide her cheeks are bound to crack. She's not much older than I am. Twenty-one or twenty-two if I had to guess. "And you must be Kasey, our newest legacy. We are so excited to have you."

I'll bet she is. She might be fooling Mom but the fake smile and high-pitched laugh is not fooling me.

"Thanks," I tell her, accepting her offered hand with a fake smile of my own.

"Hills, we're out of—" a girl says behind us but cuts herself off when she sees Hilary isn't alone. "Oh. My bad. I didn't realize you were meeting with parents today," the girl adds almost sheepishly.

I spot the empty liquor bottles in both her hands and know right away what they've recently run out of. I chance a look at my mom and wonder if she'll call the whole thing off with the obvious drinking and partying going on right now despite it only being a little after 10am on a Sunday. But instead of worry or apprehension on her face, her smile is wide, her eyes glazed over, as though she's reliving fond memories before she lets out a little laugh.

"Please, don't worry about me. You girls do what you need to. Are you over twenty-one?" Mom asks her.

"Oh, umm, I ..." She turns to Hilary with wide eyes and a *help me* expression.

Mom laughs again. "Why don't I do you girls a favor and make a quick trip to the store while you guys show my baby girl around. That looks like," she tilts her head for a better look at the bottles the newcomer is clearly trying and failing to hide, "Malibu rum, Sky Vodka, and ... is that Blue Curacao?"

The girl nods but keeps her lips sealed.

"Perfect. I'll be back in a jiff."

Mom brushes a kiss across my temple and then slips past the girl and leaves me standing alone with two very surprised college girls.

"Did your mom just—"

"Offer to go buy you booze after you very obviously failed to confirm that you're legally old enough to drink? Yes. Yes, she did."

"Wicked. Your mom is so cool."

I sigh and force myself to smile. That's Mom. Always one to be your friend rather than your parent. "Yeah. She's pretty chill. I'm Kasey by the way."

"Quinn," the girl says. "Nice to meet you."

"Let's show you around and go over the house rules while we wait for your mom to get back," Hilary interjects. "Quinn, why don't you go make sure the other pledges don't need any assistance."

Quinn nods and leaves to do what Hilary asked, and when I turn to face her, her smile is gone and an annoyed expression rests in its place. "Look," she begins. "I'm going to be honest. I wasn't thrilled when I was told we'd be admitting a new pledge. You skipped our entire application process, didn't show up for a single interview, and didn't have to jump through any of the hoops every other girl who was accepted had to."

I keep my expression blank. Is she wanting me to apologize for something I played zero part in and had no control over? It's not like I asked for this.

She sighs. "But, you're a legacy and our house takes that seriously. It also doesn't hurt that your dad made a donation to Kappa Mu in your name." Huh, look at that. Good ole Dad helping us out. I try not to roll my eyes. He was probably worried I'd ask to live with him full time what with mom leaving. Not that I ever would. I love my dad, but where Mom parents by trying to be my friend, Dad parents with assistants and nannies, forgetting I'm seventeen, not seven.

"So, we're going to make this work." She sounds resigned. Join the club. "We don't want to start getting a flood of running-start applicants. Hanging out with high schoolers isn't really our thing. We also don't want any trouble with the dean's office for exposing you to anything you're not ready for, so for now, keep your age to yourself."

"I can do that," I tell her. It's not like I was planning on letting everyone know how young I was. I'm not an idiot.

"Good. Glad that's out of the way. Like the plaque outside the door says, I'm the housemother, but I'm not going to be your mom while you're here. If you're upset or homesick, phone a friend. I'm not your shoulder to cry on."

"Noted."

"And I'm not your babysitter. The girls here like to have a bit of fun and we're close with some of the campus fraternities. You're responsible for looking after yourself. If you can't handle your liquor, don't drink. And if you do drink, don't be stupid and drive yourself home. Got it?"

I give her two thumbs up. "Anything else?"

"Don't cut classes. Part of eligibility requirements for being a member is maintaining a 3.0 GPA. If you fail any of your classes, you're out. Legacy or not."

"Good to know."

She reaches behind her and grabs an envelope from her desk before handing it to me. "Inside is a map of campus, our events schedule, and your school ID. You're required to attend all Kappa Mu functions so add these dates to your calendar. We don't make exceptions."

I tuck the envelope in the back pocket of my jeans. "Okay."
Not like I have a packed social calendar or anything. I hang
out with Allie and Bibiana on most weekends but we don't
generally plan anything official. It's usually just junk food
and movies while the guys lock themselves in the media room
to watch videos of past football games. If I have a sorority
thing, no one will care if I need to skip a night.

"Your room is on the first floor toward the back of the house.
It's just you and Quinn, the girl you just met, on this level.
Everyone else is upstairs. There's a back entrance near your
room you can use if you need to and additional parking out
back if you have a car." I nod. My dad bought me a WRX like
Aaron's, only mine is candy apple red, as a *congrats you're
going to college* gift, so that will be convenient. He's
supposed to have his driver deliver it sometime this week, so
I'll have to let him know they can bring it straight here. It'll
save me from needing a campus parking pass since I really
only plan on driving when I need to go off campus. I walk
everywhere else.

"If you have questions, check with Quinn first. All of our new
recruits are assigned a big sister. She's yours."

I nod. "Okay. Cool." Do I leave now? I'm not sure what
protocol is here exactly. Should I wait to be excused?

"That's it," Hilary confirms with a huff.

"Great. Thanks." I make a hasty retreat and wander around
downstairs, ducking around the other girls in the house until I
find a long hallway that leads to the back. I figure I'll get to

know everyone later. Right now I just want to track down my room and unpack.

The first door I find is decorated with pictures and drawings. I make a wild guess that it's Quinn's since it's her face in most of the pictures. Further down the hall are two more doors. One at the very end, which I confirm is the door that leads outside. I open it to find a small patch of grass and a concrete slab for parking on my right that leads to the main road.

I close that door and turn to the last one which I'm assuming is mine. I find Aaron lounging on my bed, phone in hand, and take in the rest of the space. It's a decent size. Double closet. I scan the room for Dominique, noting the pile of neatly stacked boxes next to the bed, half expecting him to burst from behind them just to fuck with me. "Where's Dom?" I ask when it's clear my brother isn't going to volunteer the information, too distracted by whoever he's texting with on his phone.

"Coach called. The guys had to leave for some team thing."

Relief sweeps through me and my shoulders sag. I plop down on the bed beside my brother. "I see you found my room?"

He nods, setting his phone aside. "Yeah, one of the girls told us which one was yours so we moved all your stuff in for you."

"Roman and Emilio didn't wait in the car, did they?"

He gives me a crooked grin. "Nope."

"Urgh," I groan, hiding my face with my hands. "Did anyone recognize them?"

Aaron chuckles. "Relax, sis. All they saw were some stacked guys moving boxes. No one asked if they were on the team, though Emilio definitely got his fair share of phone numbers."

I scowl. "He better have thrown them away." Emilio is a notorious flirt, but also absolutely obsessed with Bibi, his girlfriend and the mother of his child. They're doing really good, but I know Bibiana sometimes has a hard time with all the attention Emilio receives. And being a football player doesn't help. I swear all of the guys have their own personal fan clubs.

Aaron leans forward and tugs open the drawer of a nearby nightstand. Five small pieces of paper with girly handwriting in various colors greet me. "Nah, he left them for you so you could make friends. His words, not mine."

I don't bother fighting the smile that spreads over my face. That sounds like Emilio, alright.

Aaron leaves a few minutes later with the promise to help me find my classes on Monday when school starts. "Call me if you need me," he tells me on his way out, giving me a quick hug.

"I will," I promise, and then settle in and unpack my things. The room is a blank canvas. White walls, hardwood floors, and a single window that gives me a glimpse of where my car will soon be parked. There's a queen bed, a single nightstand, and a tall dresser, but nothing else aside from my boxes of belongings. I unpack my clothes first, hanging up what needs to be hung and folding everything else to add to the dresser drawers.

Mom shows up later that afternoon, her arms loaded down with shopping bags and a wide smile on her face.

"What is all that?" I ask, eyeing the pops of pink and gold peeking out the tops of the bags. I'm not a tomboy, but I'm not really a girly girl either. I played basketball throughout high school so I generally go for comfort over style. I haven't decided if I'll play this year. Coach said I could keep my spot, but a part of me would rather move beyond all things high school. I have no intention of playing in college, so stopping now wouldn't really make much difference.

"Pottery Barn was next to the grocery store so I thought I'd pick up a few things you might need. Wait until you see the comforter set I got you," she gushes, pulling out a white down comforter decorated with small pink tassels around the edge.

"Pretty," I deadpan. I'm not sure what the purpose of the tassels is but it could have been worse.

"I know, right? I wanted to make sure you were all set. I can't believe my little girl is all grown up and going to college. I know this is a big step, but I want you to know I am so proud of you."

"Thanks, Mom."

She beams. "Let's get you settled. I only have an hour before I need to get on the road, but that's plenty of time for us to turn this room into your home for the next four years."

I groan. Four years. She really expects me to be a sorority girl for all four years of college?

Her eyes soften. "I know being a Kappa Mu might not seem exciting to you right now, but honey, I made some of my very best friends in this very house when I went to college. Twenty-five years later and I'm still close with them. Sorority sisters look out for each other and you're going to meet some of the best people here. Try to be open-minded."

I sigh. "I'll try."

"Now, let's get this room situated."

4

Dominique

Roman takes off down the field and I step back with my left foot, keeping my feet staggered as I bend slightly at the knees. I raise my left arm over my shoulder, bringing the football behind my head before snapping it forward, focusing on rolling my left shoulder as I do. *Fuck.* It takes all my concentration to get the ball pointed where I need it to go.

The ball whistles through the air, heading straight for Roman, but as soon as he turns to spot the football, I realize my mistake and curse. *Too short.*

"Dammit." I kick the turf and tear off my helmet, frustration coursing through me.

Roman jerks to a stop before lunging forward to salvage the throw. He manages to catch the ball with both hands, tucking it against his chest before rolling to the ground. His momentum throws him into a complete rotation before he springs up to his feet, a bounce in his step over the save. "Fuck, yeah!" he hollers, and jogs back toward me, ball in hand.

"Not bad, man." He throws the football at me and I catch it, fingers gripping the laces.

"That was a shit throw and you know it."

He offers a noncommittal shrug. "Progress at least. And did you see that save? Perfección."

"English asshole. I'm black. Not brown like you."

He smirks. "Perfection."

True enough, and with Roman as my receiver, we have a shot at pulling this off, but it won't matter if I can't get my left arm to go the distance.

Coach called me in for an emergency meeting. I dropped E off on the way but Roman decided to tag along. Nosy bastard. The team doctor took it upon himself to inform our coach of a recent injury. Fucking snitch. If I wanted Coach to know about my shoulder, I would have told him myself.

"You could always sit this next one out," Rome offers, but I shake my head.

"You know I can't." Our second string quarterback—Deacon Hunt—is a freshman without any experience playing at this level. The guy is green. He came from a small school in the middle of nowhere and while he has a great arm, he buckles under pressure. Under normal circumstances, I wouldn't care. The point of bringing him on board is to train with him, get him where he needs to be so that by the time I graduate next year, he's ready and can lead the team. He's got potential and he needs the field time if he's going to grow, but next week we have scouts coming and they're expecting me to play.

If word gets out I'm injured and won't be on the field, there's a chance some of the scouts, maybe all, won't show. I could care less if anyone sees me play, but the other guys on the team, they need as many opportunities as they can get to shine so they have a shot at going pro. I won't be the reason they lose that.

"Let's go again," I tell Roman and he nods, getting into position, but before he starts, a voice from the sidelines draws our attention.

"Price!" Coach yells. "What the hell do you think you're doing?"

I grind my teeth together and wait as he stalks across the field like a bull. Barely six feet and thick around the middle, it's been a hot minute since the man was in his prime, but he still has no problem going toe to toe with any one of us. When he's within earshot without me needing to yell, I tell him, "Practicing, Coach."

"Practicing what, exactly? I gave you explicit orders to rest and—"

"I'm not throwing with my right," I tell him. "I'm using my left. I'll be good in time for next week's game." I have to be.

His brows pull together and I know he wants to fight me on it, but he's aware of the situation we're in just as much as I am.

"Repetitive motion tendonitis is no joke, son. If you don't take care of that arm, you can end your career before it ever starts."

"And if I don't play in next week's game, the guys on my team may find themselves in the same boat."

He takes off his red Suncrest U baseball cap and shakes his head. "They're not your responsibility. There will be more scouts, more opportunities—"

"For Davis and Elliot?" I ask, cutting him off. "They're seniors. They won't have many more chances like this." I know it. He knows it. Hell, even the guys know it, which is why so much is riding on this game. Elliot's a defensive tackle and Davis is a defensive end and they're both good. Better than good. But that won't matter if no one sees them play. They transferred in as seniors from smaller schools hoping to get some face time with scouts, but they're no-name players. Scouts aren't coming to watch them because they've never heard of them. Their best shot is to kill it on the field and have one of the already scheduled scouts recognize their potential and invite them to the NFL Scouting Combine.

Coach mutters under his breath before rubbing his jaw. "How's your right arm feel when you throw with your left?"

It twinges a bit, but I'm not telling him that. "No pain. It's all good."

He considers me for a moment. "What's your range?"

"So far, fifty-two yards," Roman answers for me.

Coach works his jaw. "How long have you been practicing?"

"Since we got out." If I had to guess, that was maybe an hour ago.

He nods to himself. "Alright. We'll try it your way. I want you out of training and practice for the next three days to rest."

I open my mouth to argue. No way can I take three days off if I'm going to get where we need me to be. We're playing Rydeville U. They're a solid team, and while I've always forced myself to throw with both arms, I'm right handed. Throwing consistently with my left isn't a cakewalk for me. I need the practice. "Coach—"

"Three days!" He waves three fingers in my face as if I need a visual. "After that, you throw and you do cardio. That's it. No weights and nothing that can strain your right shoulder. You practice with your left arm and only your left arm. I catch you so much as tossing a towel with your right and I'll bench you. Understood?"

I grit my teeth but nod. I know a losing battle when I see one. Coach is an alright guy. He puts the players' health and well-being first so I have no doubt he'll bench me, even if it means we lose next week's game.

"Good. If this is day one for you and you're already at fifty-two yards, you're ahead of Hunt. We'll make this work. But, if you have a bad performance next week, you might screw your own chances of being drafted early and some of these guys might even decide to look you over next year when the time comes. You prepared to take that risk?"

I nod. Football after college isn't in the cards for me. No matter how bad I may want it. My parents would never stand for it, and despite what some might believe, my parents do in fact have both the money and the means to ensure I go down the path they've carved out for me. This isn't one of those scenarios where I can call their bluff.

Sheridan Peretti Price and Richard Price have enough clout that they've landed themselves on the Business Insiders top ten most influential businesses in the United States six years running. As the founders of Peretti and Price, a multi-billion dollar tech company, they rub elbows with everyone from CEOs to celebrities and grossed over one hundred and eighty-two billion dollars last year alone. Yes, billion. Not million.

The amount of money my parents would need to throw around to ensure no team picked me up is barely a drop in the bucket to them. So no, I'm not worried about fucking up my own chance. I never had a real one to begin with. "It's worth the risk, Coach."

"Have it your way. Now get your asses home and rest. Valdez, keep an eye on him, and if I get wind that you or

Chavez are on the field with him these next three days, I'll make you both run so many drills you'll be begging to be benched, do I make myself clear?"

Rome nods. "Crystal."

"Good. Get out of here."

Coach stalks off the field toward the locker room and we head the opposite direction toward the parking lot. "You good, man?" Roman asks once we reach our vehicles.

I nod. "I'm good."

He hesitates, which isn't like him, so I spit out, "What?" only to see him frown.

"What was up this morning?"

"What do you mean?" I open my door and lean against the frame. I have a feeling I know where this is going and I don't like it.

"With Baby Henderson. If she'd asked us to help her move in, we would have. The girl's one of us but ..." he trails off and shakes his head, running a hand through his sweat-drenched hair.

"You're reading too much into it," I tell him, hoping he drops it.

He doesn't. "Nah. I don't think I am. Where's your head at these days? I know you had a thing for her back in high school, but—"

I cut him off before he has a chance to finish. "It's not like that. She's Aaron's little sister."

Roman snorts. "Which meant fuck all when we were in high school and you gawked at her ass every time she walked by."

"Like I said, you're reading too much into it. That was three years ago. Things change."

"Exactly. Have you seen her lately? Kasey's is all grown up and she's filled out in all the right places. Don't pretend you haven't noticed."

I lift a single brow. "Allie know you've been checking Kasey out?"

He chuckles. "No cabrón, because I'm not. But I'm not blind and neither are you. The girl has grown up. A lot. Tension with you two has always been thick, but lately ..." He trails off, giving me a knowing look.

I shake my head. "Nah, man. Things between us are not like that. I can barely stand the girl so, no, I don't fucking like her. Not the way you're suggesting. Whatever you're picking up on is just our usual shit. We get under each other's skin. That's all." I might have the occasional fantasy about fucking her to see if it would make her more tolerable, but I don't let my dick dictate my decisions.

"I was just helping Aaron out. You and E didn't have to come," I add, needing to end this conversation before he gets any ideas.

He gives me an incredulous look. "Really? That's the bullshit you're gonna try and feed me right now?"

"Drop it, man. I'm telling you, I'm not interested. Sue me. I get a kick out of riling the girl up. I saw an opportunity and I took it. That doesn't mean I want her." Though I wouldn't mind her on her knees for me, mouth open and—*Fuck. Drop that line of thinking before you get your ass in trouble.*

Roman levels me with an incredulous look. "I'm one of your best friends, cabrón. I'm not buying what you're selling. I know you better than that."

I let out a tired breath. "Ro, she's just a kid, not even eighteen yet. And you know how I am with females. You really think I'm gonna fuck myself over by trying to get a piece of her?" I shake my head. "I'm not that dumb. Allie, Bibiana, and Monique would all have my ass if I fucked things up with Kasey."

"So don't fuck it up, then. Give shit a real try. bro. You two have been going at it since senior year. You know there's something there. Everyone else can see it. Why can't you?"

"Because there isn't anything to see."

His stare is penetrating as I wait for him to concede the point.

"Is this because of Aaron?" he asks. "You know he'd come around."

"No, fucker. This is because of me. What part of 'I'm not interested' do you not understand?" He opens his mouth to argue but I cut him off. "I don't want hearts and rainbows with any female, let alone Kasey-fucking-Henderson, okay? You're wifed up and I'm happy for you, man. For E too. But I'm only interested in a tight piece of ass and a hot lay and Kasey isn't who I plan on getting that from." I make my words especially crude, hoping he gets the point. "So stop pushing. If shit changes and I decide to fuck her, I'll make sure you're the first to know."

His face hardens, and I can see the second we go from conversation mode to lecture mode. "Don't even think of going there," he warns.

"I'm not," I grind out. "You're the one suggesting—"

The lines around his mouth tighten. "If I have to kick your ass because you—"

I bark out a laugh. "Go home to your woman. Kasey's made it her mission to get under my skin. All I'm doing is returning the favor. Stop reading into nothing. We're good."

He doesn't look entirely convinced, but finally nods. "Fine. You going back to Kappa Mu?"

I should, but if I go back now, it'll give Roman the wrong idea. "Nah. I'm heading home. Gotta ice my shoulder and shit. I'll catch you later."

"Later, cabrón."

I flip off my best friend as I climb into my Escalade, put it in reverse and head for home. I pass by Greek Row and tighten my grip on the wheel until I make it to my street, three short blocks from where Kasey is living now.

Fuck. I need to get my head on straight. I'm not commitment material, and there are too many obstacles in the way, so why is it that the idea of getting past them all makes my dick twitch and brings a smile to my face?

5

Kasey

"Mom, I have to go."

"Oh, and did I tell you about the time when I was in college and—" She rattles on as though she doesn't hear me.

"Mom," I try again, shifting my bag to my other arm to avoid dropping my phone. "I'm late for class. I'll call you later. Okay?"

"Oh. Just one more thing—"

I grind my teeth together. "Mom!"

"Oh, alright. But before you hang up, can you at least tell me if you're making friends? I worry about you, sweetie." Obviously not enough since you decided to move halfway across the country.

I sigh. She means well and at least she's checking up on me. "Lots of friends. All the friends. Have to go now. Love you. Bye."

"Love yo—"

I hang up and all but run to my last class of the day, my sneakers squeaking as I race down the hallway. My phone buzzes in my hand but I send Mom to voicemail. I've talked to her three times already, and she just left for Florida yesterday. I think she's bored. It's a long drive and she still has probably a day and a half before she'll get there, assuming she doesn't stop to shop along the way.

I chance a look at the clock on my screen. *Shit.* I'm going to be late. I'm almost to the door when another figure turns the corner on my right and crashes into me.

I drop my bag and my books tumble out onto the floor. My body sways with my momentum, but the stranger reaches out, grabbing me with an iron grip before I land face first on the linoleum. "Ow. Crap."

"Watch where you're going," the guy snaps.

Asshole. I jerk my arm free and ignore him, not bothering to look up. This is just my luck. I drop to the floor to grab my things, conscious of the time as I rush to put everything back in my bag. I'm so screwed. It's only the second day of school and I'm going to be late to my english class for the second day in a row.

His feet edge closer. Black Beast Mode sneakers come into my line of vision, making me think of the red ones Dominique wears. *Urgh, and now I'm thinking about Dominique.*

The guy crouches down and retrieves my last book before handing it to me. "Sorry. I didn't mean to snap at you. You just came out of nowhere. I'm late to my English class and my professor is known to be a real hardass. I didn't mean to take you out like that."

I accept the book, rising to my feet and finally look up at the stranger beside me. Honey-colored eyes framed with dark brows meet mine. I suck in a breath, my heart skipping a beat. I'm taken aback by my response to him, but the longer I stare makes me realize I'm not that surprised.

He's gorgeous in a devastating way. Medium brown skin, full lips. I wouldn't say he's light skinned, but he's not as dark as Dominique. He's wearing slim-fitting jeans that are torn in the knees and a long white crew shirt that molds to his body. Add to that the black sneakers and a black ball cap turned backwards and he's stunning. I'm not sure how else to describe him.

Most of the skin I can see on him is covered in ink. Two forearm sleeves disappear beneath the long sleeves of his shirt that he's pushed up to his elbows, and he has a cross tattoo on the left side of his neck. A scroll design filled with script on his right.

But despite looking like Kelly Oubre Jr's doppelganger, there's something about the way he's studying me that sets me on edge.

"It's fine. Sorry for slamming into you," I say.

The corners of his mouth curl into a calculated smirk. He licks his lips and rubs his palms together, almost like a prayer. "Nothing to be sorry about." His eyes roam over me, sliding down from my face, lingering on my chest, and then returning to my face again.

"Alrighty then." I move to step around him but he mirrors my steps, effectively blocking me.

What is he doing?

"You have Fisks for English 101, right? I saw you in the back the other day." His eyes rake me over in appreciation once again. He's not even trying to hide his interest.

Normally, I'd be flattered, but right now I just want to get to class.

"Um. Yeah." I tuck a piece of hair behind my ear and try to ignore the way my stomach clenches. "So you know, gotta run."

I try to go around him again but his hand shoots out, gripping my forearm. "Hold up," his voice pitches low and his eyes lock onto mine.

Mine widen, a flash of trepidation slamming into me before I shove it aside. I don't know who this guy thinks he is, but he can't just grab me. I tug on my arm, but unlike the first time, he doesn't release me. His fingers flex, his grip tightening as his penetrating stare bores into me. Something dark and dangerous seeps into his expression and tension bleeds into the air.

I swallow hard. My gaze darts around us, taking in the empty hallway. Classes started almost over five minutes ago, so it's just the two of us in the halls.

He must pick up on my anxiety because all of a sudden the dark look on his face is gone, replaced with an easy carefree grin. "Safety in numbers, right? Come on." Not giving me a chance to respond he gives me a conspiratorial wink and pulls me the rest of the way to our class, his hand wrapped around me though they've slipped down, his fingers encircling my wrist.

The door to our class is already closed but he quietly inches it open and peers inside.

"How's it look?" I ask, trying to dispel some of the tension still thick between us. I attempt to peer over his shoulder, but he's nearly a foot taller than me so I can't see much.

He turns to look at me, giving me another smile, and I realize he's young. Probably a freshman like me since we're in the same English class. He still has some softness to his face, though that looks like the only place you would find any. His shoulders are broad, his waist narrow and his arms are corded with muscle. Between the body, the arrogance, and the shoes, I'm betting he's an athlete, and since Beast Mode Gear is owned by a former NFL player, I'll assume he's on the football team.

"Come on," he whispers, tugging me through the door with him. He adjusts his hold again, this time capturing my hand with his. I stare at our laced fingers with a frown, but allow him to lead me inside so as not to disturb the class.

Fisks is at the whiteboard, his back to us as he writes today's assignment on the board. We get a few interested looks from other students as we make our way to the empty seats in the back, my hand still locked in his as he raises his finger to his lips, the universal sign to be quiet. A few students nod and grin before turning their attention back to the front of the class.

Once safely in our seats, he releases me and I expel a relieved breath right as our professor turns around to face the class. His gaze lands on me and he frowns but doesn't comment, continuing with his lecture.

"That was a close one," the guy who crashed into me says.

I bite my bottom lip and nod. Pulling out my notebook so I can take notes on today's lecture, I do my best to block out our strange encounter, hoping that's the end of it.

"I'm Deacon," he whispers, eyes straight ahead as though paying attention to Mr. Fisks.

I don't bother to respond. But after a minute passes, he asks, "What's your name?"

I consider refusing to answer, but what would be the point? It wouldn't be hard to figure out if he really wanted to.

"Kasey," I whisper under my breath.

"Nice to—"

"Mr. Hunt."

Deacon tilts his head to our professor, adopting a bored expression. "Yeah?"

"Is there something you'd like to share with the class?" Mr. Fisks asks, and there's a warning in his voice.

"Nah, I'm good," Deacon answers, unconcerned.

"Then I suggest you pay attention to today's lesson. We'll have an exam this Friday." He turns away, droning on about what will be covered on the exam and this week's assigned reading, but I'm not really paying attention. I glance at Deacon through my peripheral, only to catch his eyes on mine.

He reaches into his backpack and retrieves a notebook of his own. His large dark hands make it impossible for me to see what he's writing, but I know it's not anything class related.

He tugs on the page, tearing it out before neatly folding it in half and sliding it onto my desk with an arrogant smirk.

I purse my lips and give him a questioning look. One he returns with a wink. Rolling my eyes, I reach for the note and carefully unfold it so as not to draw Mr. Fisk's attention again.

A laugh bubbles up in my throat and I cover it with a cough when I see what the note says.

He wrote, **Will you go out with me?** on the page in tight neat letters, much neater than I would have expected from a guy, with three check boxes beneath the question labeled, **Yes. No.** And **Maybe.**

My shoulders shake as I struggle to contain a snicker. This guy, is he for real? What are we, five?

I reach for my pen and check the No box before adding a thank you beside it and discreetly passing it back to him.

He opens the note and scowls, his expression a split between genuine surprise and confusion, before he writes something else, his strokes almost aggressive before he folds in the paper in half and passes it back.

Why not?

I chew on my bottom lip. Because you manhandled me. Because there is something about you that screams danger: proceed with caution. And even if none of those things were true, he probably plays football for Suncrest U, which adds two more strikes against him. The first because he's most likely a total player, and the second because that makes him teammates with Roman, Emilio, and Dominique and yeah, that is just a disaster waiting to happen. Aaron's my big brother, but those three can take overprotective to the extreme.

Somehow writing any of that down seems like a bad idea, so instead I write, **I don't know you. What if you're a crazy stalker?**

I pass the note back to him and he makes quick work of his response.

No stalker tendencies present. I'm a nice guy. Promise. I give him a dubious look and he raises his little finger in the universal gesture for a pinkie swear.

"I'm not sure I believe you," I whisper while making sure our teacher isn't looking my way.

His brows pull together. "That I'm a nice guy or that I'm not a stalker?"

I shrug. I mean, really, it could go either way.

He huffs out a breath and snatches the paper off my desk, writing furiously before handing it back, but instead of slipping it on my desk he holds it out between us, his entire attention on me as he waits for me to take it.

A few of our classmates are giving us interested looks, but I ignore them and focus on the boy beside me. He raises his brows and waves the paper in his hand.

Urgh, fine. I hold my hand out and he slowly places it in the palm of my hand, his fingers trailing across my skin before he withdraws. I shiver.

Give me a chance. I can see I made a shitty first impression. Let me fix that.

I fight back an eye roll before scribbling across the paper and handing it back.

What sort of date? I ask.

The corner of his mouth quirks. **Pizza and a movie at my place?** he answers.

Pass. I just met the guy and he expects me to go back to his place with him on the first date? Do I have booty call stamped on my forehead somewhere or something?

Netflix and chill? Not really my thing. I write and toss the note back to him. We're running out of space to write so hopefully this will end soon because his date suggestion only confirms that he is a total player who wants an easy lay. *Sorry, buddy. That isn't me.* Then again, what did I expect? He probably has his own personal fan club of jersey chasers who are happy to throw their panties at him.

The note lands on my desk again. **Not what I meant. I figured we could do something low key. Get to know each other.** When he puts it like that, it doesn't sound *so bad,* but it's still bad and I'm not naive enough to fall for it.

Dominique's face flashes through my mind. His lips pressed into a disapproving frown, a silent warning that I better fucking not. My stomach flip flops which only serves to annoy me more. I shake the image of him from my head. *What the hell is wrong with me? I shouldn't care whether or not Dominique would approve. Actually, I don't care. Not one bit.* This is just a side effect of sleep deprivation. I barely slept last night. Whoever is in the room over mine decided to have company over, and let's just say they stayed up into the wee morning hours doing some extracurricular activities, and had zero problem letting the entire house know about it. Yeah, that's all it is. I just need to catch up on sleep.

I give Deacon another look through my peripheral. He gives me a small smile and a tilt of his head as if to say *please.*

I'm not really looking to get into a relationship. I write, and return the paper to him, somewhat frustrated at my unwillingness to give the guy a shot. I know Dominique is factoring into that decision, even if he isn't the only reason, and I hate it. Hate that he has this invisible pull over me when I know nothing will ever happen between us, and that's a good thing. We can hardly stand one another.

Deacon's mouth dips down as he writes out his response.

Not asking for your hand in marriage or to be your boyfriend. Just a chance to get to know you. Maybe be friends?

Friends wouldn't be a horrible idea, but ... I mentally shake myself. I might regret this, but I refuse to let Dominique's imaginary disapproval decide for me. **Okay. Friends.**

His smile grows when he sees my answer. **Any suggestions for our first friend date?**

Not a date. But how about coffee?

Got it. What's your number?

We exchange phone numbers and I discreetly enter his into my phone, praying this isn't a mistake when the teacher draws everyone's attention.

"That'll be all for today. Finish your reading for the week and do not forget about Friday's exam. This will count for twenty percent of your grade, so it would behoove you not to slack off. It will be difficult to catch up should you fail and there will not be retakes so don't think emailing me you're sick the night before will buy you any extra time to study. It won't."

A collective groan rolls through the class as everyone shuffles to their feet. "So," Deacon rubs the back of his neck. "What class do you have next?"

"Health," I tell him as we both walk out the door. His hand brushes against mine and I instinctively bring it to my chest. He doesn't notice my reaction.

"Cool. I'll walk with you. I'm going the same way."

"Sure." I mean, it is a free country. I can't very well tell him, no.

We spend the next ten minutes talking about nothing and everything, and my initial apprehension begins to wane. Deacon is ... charismatic. He's animated when he talks, using his hands, and his face is so expressive. He's one hundred percent as arrogant as I initially pegged him to be but, I don't know, he's not an asshole about it, despite what happened in the hallway, and he doesn't grab me again.

I find myself laughing more than I'm used to after meeting someone new. There's just something about talking to him that is, I don't know, easy. He reminds me a lot of Emilio in that way.

I discover Deacon is in fact on the football team. No surprise there. He's second string seeing as he's an incoming freshman, and he's a QB so he's gunning for Dominique's spot.

He's confident and definitely a little cocky that he'll get it by the end of the year, but I know that won't happen. Not before Dominique graduates at least, so Deacon will have to wait until his junior year to start.

A part of me wonders if the two of them are friends, or friendly at least, since Dominique would be the one responsible for working with him. None of the guys are particularly social unless they have to be, Dominique less so than even Roman, and that's saying something.

In high school, the guys actively avoided everyone not in their close-knit circle, including their fellow teammates, and were called Devils for a reason that had nothing to do with the school mascot and everything to do with the hell they rained down on anyone dumb enough to bother them.

I can't imagine things are any different here. It's unlikely Dominique would bother getting to know a second-string player off the field, but during training and practices, he might be less of an asshole. Maybe. Okay, probably not, but a part of me is tempted to ask Deacon how well he knows

Dominique. I try not to dwell on why I want to know that, though.

We reach the school's athletic center and I turn to wave goodbye.

"See you around, Deacon," I tell him, but before I can move for the doors, he clasps my hand with his and tugs just enough to stop me.

"Okay, can you not do that?" I ask.

He drops my hand immediately, lifting his own in a show of surrender. "My bad. I just ..." He adopts a sheepish expression. "I wanted you to know, I'm glad we ran into each other today. Literally and figuratively." He drops his hands and a slow smile spreads across his face."You're not like other girls, Kasey. It's refreshing."

Oh.

"Thanks. I, uh, I'm glad we ran into each other too."

"Yeah?" he asks.

I roll my eyes. "Yeah. You're not that bad, but don't let it go to your head. I've only agreed to coffee," I remind him, and the next thing I know, he closes the distance between us, reclaiming my hand anyway as he brings it to his mouth, gently pressing his lips to my knuckles.

His eyes flick up, holding my gaze, and a small smile plays on his lips before he straightens and takes a step back. "See you around, *friend.*"

"Yep." I turn and make a beeline for the doors, not sure what to think of that, when for the second time today I crash into another warm body, this time hard enough that I stumble back a few steps and fall flat on my butt.

"Seriously!"

A warm chuckle has me looking up to find Dominique's amused stare locked on me. Not who I wanted to run into right now.

6

Kasey

"Where's the fire?" he asks, peering down at me like the brooding asshole I know him to be.

I open my mouth to snap at him for being a jerk and letting me fall, because I know he did it on purpose. Dominique's reflexes are lightning fast, so there is zero doubt in my mind he could have prevented my fall if he'd wanted to. But before I snap at him, his gaze shifts past me to the doors, a frown marring his face and a flash of anger ignites in his eyes.

I turn, but no one is there. I wonder if he saw me talking to Deacon. If he did, does he care? Probably not. But then why would he be angry?

I shove myself to my feet, dusting my hands on the back of my jeans. "Thanks for the save," I mock.

His attention turns back to me. "Why were you walking with Hunt?" he asks, his gaze probing.

"Who?"

"Hunt?" At my blank look he huffs. "Deacon Hunt. The guy you were talking to on your way over here. Why were you talking to him?"

"Am I not supposed to?" I ask, not bothering to answer his question as I head to my next class. I have ten minutes before it starts, but I'd rather Dominique think I don't have time to talk at the moment. Instead of dropping it, though, he falls into step beside me, his long strides eating through the distance and instinctively making me speed up until I realize what I'm doing and force myself to slow down.

"He's on the team," he says and his frown deepens. He slows down once he sees I'm no longer beside him.

"Why is that a problem? You, Roman, and Emilio are all on the team too."

We walk in silence together for several minutes before he finally says, "It's not the same."

I bark out a laugh. "I'm sorry. How exactly is it different?"

He glowers down at me, but I refuse to be affected.

"You know what jocks are like. They're not better in college than they were in high school. They're worse."

I roll my eyes. "Yes, I'm well aware. I have three guy friends who are damn near football gods with a well-established reputation for being man-whoring assholes. Luckily, two met the girls of their dreams and have since been reformed, the third..." I make a show of thinking it over, tapping my finger against my lower lip. "The third is still up to his asshole man-whoring ways. It's sad, actually. He's a bit of a lost cause."

Dominique's gaze sharpens. "I'm not a man-whore."

I snort. "At least you don't deny you're an asshole."

His teeth grind together. I struck a nerve with that one.

"I don't have to explain myself to you."

"Ding. Ding. Ding. You are one hundred percent right."

His eyes widen the smallest amount, but it's enough to relay his surprise at my words. Oh, he made this too easy and doesn't even realize it yet.

"And I should respect that. So, I will. And since you brought it up, you must also know that I don't need to explain myself to you, either." I grin, my smile widening the darker and more hooded his expression gets.

I know Mom always said you should never poke a bear, but I don't think she realized just how much fun it could be.

A growly sound rumbles deep in his chest.

"He's a player."

I shrug my shoulders. "Cool. I don't really care."

"You don't."

I roll my eyes. "Why would I?" I've already decided I'm not dating the guy, so it's a non-issue.

Dominique goes quiet again before he barks out a mocking laugh. Shaking his head, his mouth curls into a cruel smile, the one he seems to wear more and more whenever I'm around. "I shouldn't be surprised."

I frown. "Surprised by what?" I ask and then kick myself for being so damn predictable. The smart move would have been to ignore his comment. Not to play right into his hands.

His eyes burn with thinly veiled hostility. "That you've become like every other chick on campus. Both stupid and shallow if you're willing to date a known player to gain a little bit of popularity." He shakes his head as though I've somehow disappointed him. "I thought you were better than that." He shrugs. "Guess I was wrong."

I ignore his stab, but then he decides to cut a little deeper. "I give you a month. Maybe two before he cheats." His gaze rakes over me, but there isn't a hint of desire in his eyes as they travel over my body. Instead, they hold mock pity and disgust. "On second thought, just the one. He'll lose interest before you hit the second."

My cheeks heat and I know he can see the blush climbing up my neck.

"Fuck you." My words shake as I clench my hands into tight fists at my side. Why did that hurt so much?

He grunts. "Pass."

Fury spikes my bloodstream, my anger and humiliation at his words filling me like a vicious, violent wave. I don't even realize what's happening until it's done. One second I'm about to storm off and the next, my fist is flying, connecting with his jaw, but only enough to graze it because dammit, he's too fucking tall.

The next thing I know Dominique is shoving me into an empty classroom. The door closes behind us and he locks it before pressing me back into the nearest wall. I suck in a breath and Dominique lifts both arms on either side of me, caging me in with his bulk. "That was an incredibly stupid thing to do." I don't miss the threat in his voice, but I absolutely choose to ignore it.

I fist both hands in the fabric of his shirt and shove him with all of my strength, but it's like trying to move a mountain. "I always knew you were a jerk. But I never knew you were this cruel."

"It can't be considered cruelty if it's the truth."

Tears sting the backs of my eyes before I blink them away. "Never let them see you cry, sweetheart," Mom used to tell me. When Dad left her and filed for divorce, it was the lowest I'd ever seen her, but she never did let him see her cry. She was strong. And she raised me to be strong too. I refuse to break down and cry in front of Dominique all because what? He hurt my feelings? Fuck that. His opinion means nothing to me.

"Well, thanks for clearing that up." My lower lip trembles until I sink my teeth into it, using the pain as an anchor.

Dominique is silent as he stares down his nose at me, eyes devoid of emotion.

"I fucking hate you," I tell him.

Zero reaction.

"You said your piece. Told me I'm stupid and shallow and can't hold a guy's attention. Is there anything else you need to get off your chest? I have a class to get to, and this right here," I wave my arm between us, "is a waste of my time."

His gaze latches onto my arm.

With surprising speed and gentle hands he lifts my arm up, bringing it closer to his face like he's looking for—

I mutter out a curse seeing what caught his attention. Light bruises in the shape of fingers wrap around my forearm. Shit.

Dominique's expression goes from blank to murderous as he grinds out his next words. "Who touched you?" His already dark brown eyes turn even darker, sending a shiver down my spine.

I don't answer him.

"I'm not going to ask again, Kasey. Who. Fucking. Touched. You?"

7

Dominique

My nostrils flare taking in the yellow and purple bruise on Kasey's fair skin. There's no mistaking that it's from a hand. The shape is too distinct, and the imprint is large. A man's. Someone hurt her.

Whoever he is, he's a dead man.

Kasey's already pale skin has gone two shades paler, making her bright blue eyes damn near glow. Her mouth parts, tongue peeking out to lick her full bottom lip. My dick twitches and I silently curse, willing it to stand the fuck down.

She swallows hard, and I know her mind is racing for a response.

"Don't even think about lying to me," I warn.

In a move I never would have expected from her, Kasey twists her arm out of my grasp and dips beneath the arm I have pressed against the wall caging her in, in a desperate attempt at escape. It takes two seconds for her hand to reach the door, but before she can open it, I catch her by the waist and tug her back against me. "Not so fast, baby girl."

Her anger and hatred for me roll off her in waves as she digs her short nails into my arms and kicks her legs, cursing my name.

I flip her around and press her against the door, using my body to pin her in place. I've tried to keep myself in check, but she is not making this shit easy.

"Get off of me," she shouts, and I cover her mouth with my palm, my hand so large I damn near cover half her face. Fuck she's small. Fragile.

Her eyes blaze and I lean in, ensuring she sees that I am not fucking around right now. Not when it comes to something like this.

"Don't you dare open that pretty little mouth of yours and scream like that again. Do you feel me? Unless you're ready to tell me who the fuck was dumb enough to touch you, or decide to drop down on your knees and wrap your lips around my cock, your mouth is going to stay closed."

Her eyes narrow, nostrils flaring. She's so fucking pissed, and I wish I had more time to enjoy it. I've worked hard this past year getting Kasey to hate me. It makes keeping her out of my bed a hell of a lot easier that way. But damn if seeing her like this doesn't make my dick hard, and the thought of her on her knees for me ... *fuck*. I can't be the only one affected by that image.

Her small fingers wrap around my wrist, pulling to get my hand off of her mouth.

"Are you going to behave?"

If looks could kill I'd be dead right now with the way she's glaring at me.

"It's a yes or no question, baby girl. Blink twice for yes. Once for no."

Her eyes narrow. Seconds pass and the air grows impossibly thick. I'm sure she can feel my hard-on pressed against her stomach, but neither of us is going to acknowledge it.

When a full minute has passed, she blinks twice and concedes. A rush of satisfaction swells inside my chest. I drop my hand, but don't step away. I rationalize that the moment I do she'll bolt. It has nothing to do with how fucking good she feels with her tight little body up against mine. Her lips are pressed into a thin line, her cheeks scarlet. A mix of anger and indignation. She is so fucking beautiful like this.

A few strands of her blond hair fell from her hair tie during our struggle and I slowly reach out, tucking the flyaways behind her ear. Her eyes are guarded as I trail one finger down the side of her face before cupping her jaw. She closes her eyes, a small shudder moving through her.

"What's his name, Kasey?" I ask, and there's a bite of steel in my tone.

Her eyes snap open and she bears her teeth. "You're making a big deal out of nothing. It was an accide—"

"No man leaves a mark on a female by accident." My voice is deceptively calm. I lean down closer to her until our breaths mingle. "Was it Hunt? Did he do that?" The sudden widening of her eyes gives her away, and my vision goes red.

My jaw flexes and I go to step back but she latches onto me, wrapping her arms around my neck. "Whatever it is you're thinking of doing, don't. It was an accident. I don't think he meant to hurt me." I fight the urge to encircle her waist and rise to my full height, taking her with me.

Her arms tighten as her feet lift from the ground. "Dominique—"

"You can't protect your boyfriend," I tell her. "Not from this."

Her feet sway off the floor and her arms tighten around my neck, squeezing to maintain her hold on me since I haven't bothered to help her out.

"He's not my boyfriend. We literally just met because I slammed into him running late to class." My pulse jumps at her words. "I don't even know the guy. We have one class together and this is the first time we've spoken."

I grab the backs of her thighs, hoisting her higher up. Her legs wrap around my waist and my hands move to her ass. I lean her back against the door and wait to see if she'll demand to be put down. She doesn't. Neither does she yell at me for the way I'm cupping her ass right now.

"If you're protecting him—"

She snorts. "I'm not. I have no reason to, so get off your high horse. I'm not some damsel in need of saving."

"Is that so?" I ask, shifting my hips so her center grinds down on my cock.

She gasps. "What are you doing?"

I repeat the movement, and she shakes in my arms. "Are you sure you're not in need of saving?"

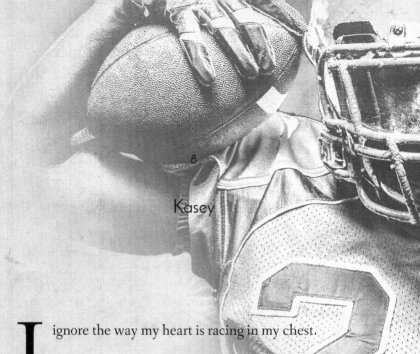

I ignore the way my heart is racing in my chest.

"By the guy who just called me stupid, shallow, and implied I was unattractive and incapable of holding a man's attention?" I shake my head. "I think I'm good."

There's a flash of something in his gaze I can't quite put my finger on. His hold tightens on my ass and his dick strains against his jeans, pressing firmly between my thighs. What was I thinking wrapping my legs around him like this?

As if hearing my thoughts, Dominique smirks. *Asshole.* I decide to give him a taste of his own medicine.

Using his shoulders for leverage I raise myself up a few inches and roll my hips over his length in a long caress. He sucks in a breath, his eyes dark and filled with challenge.

Holding his stare, I do it again, and his entire body trembles with need. I'm not blind. Despite his earlier words, he wants me. He won't after today, but right now at this very moment, Dominique Price wants to fuck me, and knowing that sends a flood of euphoria surging through me. This means he's no longer in control here. I'm the one with all the power now.

"Don't start something you can't finish."

"Why not? It's not like you could possibly want me, right? So why would me doing this," I grind my pussy against him again, liquid heat soaking my panties, "matter to you? You can't possibly be affected, right?"

He doesn't say a word, but when I give another deliberate roll of my hips, he digs his fingers into my ass and thrusts upward, grinding his dick into me in response.

To my complete horror, a moan escapes me, and he levels me with a knowing smirk.

I dig my short nails into his shoulders as he dry humps me against the classroom door in long languid thrusts and Oh. My. God. That feels good.

One of his hands comes up to knead my breast and I shamelessly arch into his touch. He grunts against the corner of my mouth and the sound snaps something in me, lifting some of the pleasure-induced haze from my eyes.

Why do I let him make me feel like this? I fucking hate him.

Taking a deep breath, I lean forward, licking and biting my way up his neck until my lips graze the shell of his ear. "What would you do if I told you to fuck me?" I whisper and swirl my tongue along his skin.

His sharp intake of breath lets me know I've surprised him and he freezes, pulling back just enough to meet my gaze. His eyes are drowning in need, but there's a hint of confusion too, so I decide to taunt him some more. I make a show of licking my lips and his eyes immediately drop to my mouth.

"You'd like that, wouldn't you?"

He doesn't answer, but his muscles strain against his skin, the veins in his neck protruding.

"I bet you'd like it even more if I begged for it. Got down on my knees and showed you just how bad I—"

His fist tangles in my hair and he yanks my face toward his, tilting my head so his lips can capture my own. His kiss is savage and hungry as he claims my mouth with his tongue in long greedy stokes. I moan into his mouth, and that only seems to spur him on.

His grip holds me in place, leaving me no choice but to accept his punishing kiss. The hand in my hair moves to the side of my neck in a possessive hold while the other continues to hold me up, kneading my ass. He pulls away from the door and carries me further into the room, his mouth never leaving mine until I feel a solid surface beneath me.

Dominique sets me down on a long table, but he doesn't release me. "That what you want?" he asks, and it takes me a few seconds to remember what I said to him before that kiss. "You want me to fuck you while you beg for my cock?"

God, yes. Not that I'll ever admit it out loud. Instead, I lean back, pressing my palms on the table to hold myself up. His hand slips from my neck right as I say, "No thanks. I think I'm good."

I allow a smirk to curl the corners of my mouth as I raise both brows, giving him a disinterested look.

He glares at me in disbelief and then something in him shifts. Tension crackles like lightning between us, and I fight not to squirm under his intense stare.

"You almost had me," he tsks with an amused laugh. "Almost. But if you think for one second I'm going to buy that mouthful of lies, guess again, baby girl." He steps into me, cupping my sex and driving the heel of his palm against me. "You're soaked pussy doesn't lie. I can feel how wet you are through your jeans."

My eyes pop wide and my heart beats frantically against my chest before I can pull myself together enough to bite out, "Screw you."

"You'd like that wouldn't you?" He smirks, palm still pressed firmly against my center. My hips lift off the table of their own volition when he pushes down on my clit. I gasp, biting back a moan, and my cheeks burn with humiliation, but I can't find it in me to tell him to stop. It feels so good.

"I don't like liars," he grunts, his eyes locked on his hand between my legs. *Wait. What?* He drags my hips to the edge of the table until my butt is about to slide off. Then he spreads my legs, creating enough room for him to step between them. He makes no effort to mask his desire as he slams his lips down on mine again and groans into my mouth right before he fists my hair and jerks my head back, tearing his lips from mine and leaving me to stare up at the ceiling. He scrapes his teeth along the column of my throat, nipping and sucking on my sensitive skin.

I gasp, and a fresh wave of pleasure filters through me, igniting every cell in my body.

He runs his nose up the side of my neck, inhaling me as he says, "So, I have to punish you." There's a note of regret in his voice, and the next thing I know, he's spun me around to face the opposite wall. My feet hit the floor, my body bent over the desk and my ass thrust out toward him. One hand presses down on the center of my spine, effectively pinning me in place as the other roams over my hip, trailing down to my ass.

"What am I being punished for?" My heart rate picks up.

"You lied to me."

I shake my head in denial. "I didn't lie." My voice shakes, but whether from desire or fear, I'm not entirely sure.

"There you go again," he tsks.

His hand dips lower, boldly stroking the inside of my thighs as he uses his legs to force me into a wider stance. I grind my teeth together to hold back the moan that threatens to spill past my lips.

"I'm going to give you a second chance to come clean, because despite what you think, I'm not a complete asshole."

I start to laugh, but the sound dies in my throat when I feel the ridge of his cock dig into my ass, hard and demanding. What is he doing to me? We don't get along. We definitely don't like one another. But the level of need I feel right now is like nothing I've felt before, which is both exhilarating and terrifying at the same time because this is bad. So fucking bad.

"Do you want me to fuck you, baby girl?" My mouth goes dry as he thrusts against me, pressing his cock against the crack of my ass as he mimics fucking me. "Do you want to beg for my cock as I thrust deep inside you?"

My pussy clenches and his vulgar words almost undo me. I swallow hard and manage to deliver a shaky denial, "No."

He stops moving and exhales a sigh full of resignation, as if my response somehow pains him. "I did warn you," he says, his voice tinged with regret.

I swallow hard, wondering what he intends to do next. I've never seen him like this. He's always been so restrained. We fight, sure, but with words. This isn't anything like our usual battles. This is like going to war and I am wholly outmatched and unprepared for this kind of fight.

One hand reaches around me and undoes the button on my jeans. "Last chance," he offers, but words die on my tongue. My thighs tighten in anticipation. Is he...are we going to...

His fingers hook into my jeans, dragging them over my hips and exposing my rear. He leaves my underwear in place, but all

I'm wearing is a hot pink thong that leaves my entire backside on display. "Fuck," he groans and cups my ass cheeks, spreading them with his fingers while also pushing me forward, father across the table until the tops of my thighs can't go any further.

"Tell me to stop," he growls. "If you're not okay with this, whatever the fuck is about to happen right now, tell me now." He runs his fingers down the crack of my ass until he reaches my pussy and presses his fingers into me through the soaked fabric of my panties. My legs quake.

I should do what he suggests, tell him to stop, but I'm drunk on desire, feeling like I'll explode if he stops touching me, so I keep my lips pressed together and shake my head. I'll regret this come morning.

I won't be able to pretend this didn't happen. I won't be able to forget his hands on me or the sensation of him thrusting between my thighs. This is a mistake and I know it. I just don't fucking care.

Dominique twists his hand in my hair and I instinctively know what comes next. It's no surprise when he yanks on it, forcing my back to arch and my chin to jut forward. He seems to like that, pulling my hair. And I can't say that I'm complaining about it.

I don't have a lot of experience in this arena. I've fooled around before, sure. Given head. Had my pussy eaten out. But I haven't gone all the way with anyone. I'm not saving myself for marriage or anything like that, I just never cared about any of my past boyfriends enough to spread my legs for them.

I've never been with a guy like this. One who my body responds to on a visceral level.

Dom shifts to the side, no longer between my thighs, but he doesn't let go of my hair. He winds it around his fist, tightening his hold as his other hand hooks beneath the fabric of my panties and a lone finger slips between my wet slit.

I moan when he finds my clit, brushing his finger over the sensitive nub.

"Dominique ..." I gasp, and his finger moves faster against me, my hips rearing back of their own accord. The pain in my scalp and the pleasure between my thighs has pure heat zipping down my spine. My toes curl and I'm panting heavy, my release so incredibly close.

"Don't say I didn't warn you," he mutters under his breath right before he withdraws his finger from between my legs and his palm slaps my bare ass cheek. I yelp, jolting forward, but the table makes it impossible to go anywhere.

Holy fuck. "Did you just spank me?"

Instead of answering, he spanks my other cheek and I slap my palm against the table.

"I warned you what would happen if you didn't tell the truth." He massages my burning flesh, lessening the sting a bit, only to slap me again. I cry out, but the sound is cut off when he releases my hair only to wrap his hand over my mouth.

"Shhhh...." he whispers. "Keep making that sound and someone is bound to come and investigate what is going on in here."

I try to shift away from him. When he said he was going to punish me for lying, I didn't expect this.

He chuckles, like my attempt at escape amuses him. "I'm not done with you yet. I think you deserve at least two more." A fourth smack is delivered and I scream, but his palm muffles the sound.

"Your ass turns the prettiest shade of pink," he tells me, and I whimper against his palm.

He squeezes my ass, trailing his fingers over each cheek and between my cleft. He said two more, but he's only delivered one, and the anticipation of what is still to come grips my chest.

Dominique lets go of my mouth and shifts behind me, pressing his erection against me. "Want to try again?" he asks, rocking his hips against me. "Tell me the truth and maybe I'll consider giving you what you want. Beg for my cock the way we both know you want to."

The smug sound of his voice has my eyes narrowing and I lift my head to look over my shoulder. I won't beg for anything. Not from him or anyone else. My gaze collides with his and just as I open my mouth to tell him to fuck off, his palm slaps my ass, harder than all of the times before.

I open my mouth on a silent scream before sucking in a shaky breath as I sag against the table.

Dominique steps back, moving around the table until he's standing in front of me, able to meet my gaze. He casually leans forward, pushing the hair out of my face. I should stand up. At the very least pull my jeans back over my ass, but I can't seem to find the energy to move.

"You know, you're not nearly as insufferable when you're like this."

I raise one hand and flip him off.

He laughs and then, unsurprisingly, walks out of the classroom without so much as a goodbye.

9

Dominique

I left Kasey bare-assed in that classroom. Aaron's little sister. Ass cheeks red, courtesy of yours truly, and on display for anyone who walked in to see. This is bad. Already, there is a voice in my head that whispers *you traitor, he's like a brother. He trusts you.*

There's a lead weight in my gut. I shouldn't have touched her. I sure as shit shouldn't still be thinking about touching her.

Thank God I didn't go through with fucking her. Not that what I did do constitutes as much better. A heavy blanket of guilt encompasses me. This can't happen again. Me. Her. I lied when I told Roman I wasn't interested. What I meant was I can't afford to be interested. Not in her. Not like that.

I reach the locker room and make quick work of changing. I'm a few minutes late, but no one will care. I'm not practicing today, still on Coach's mandatory rest period for my shoulder, but that doesn't mean I'm gonna bounce on my obligations. Or miss the chance to give Deacon a piece of my mind.

Kasey might say it was an accident, but I'm not buying it.

Seeing that bruise on her arm ... I shake my head and take a deep breath. It damn near sent me over the edge. The thought of anyone hurting her, anyone who isn't me—and yeah, I realize how fucked up that is—makes my blood boil.

I want to fuck her. Punish her. Soothe her. I want her to ache because of me and I want to be the only one capable of taking that ache away.

Smacking her ass and watching it redden has blood rushing straight to my cock. Seeing her lust-drenched eyes, feeling just how soaking wet her panties are, *shit,* it does something to me.

The door leading to the field opens and Emilio walks in, shouting, "Yeah, yeah. I'll be back. Chill the fuck out," over his shoulder.

"It's about time you showed up. Everything good?" he asks, seeing me on the bench.

I grunt. "Peachy."

He opens his locker, the one right next to mine, and gives me a curious look.

"What'd you do?" he asks.

"What are you talking about?"

He grabs a roll of athletic tape and begins wrapping his wrists. "You look guilty as fuck, man. Where were you before you got here?"

I keep my expression blank. "I think you've been watching too many *telenovelas* with Bibiana, E."

He chuckles. "You got me there, but bro, Señora Acero is savage. That opening scene is *a la Game of Thrones* two-thousand thirteen. A wedding. A massacre. You don't know what you're missing."

"I'll take your word for it."

He finishes with his wrists and tosses the tape back in his locker. "I still can't believe you stopped watching at the ten-minute mark." He shakes his head. "Fifteen more minutes and it would have gotten to the good part."

"I couldn't understand anything."

Emilio scoffs. "Turn on the fucking subtitles. It's fine."

I stretch my back and put myself through a short series of stretches as we bullshit a little longer. I know what I'm planning to do once I walk out on the field, but what I don't know is how to get Emilio and Roman off of it.

"Hunt," I shout, ensuring my voice carries across the field. His head jerks up and he looks around, searching for whoever called his name. As soon as he realizes it was me, he jogs his way over, pulling off his helmet once he's close.

"Yo. What's up?" He tilts his head in greeting, wiping the sweat from his brow with the back of his arm.

"Kasey Henderson." I bite out her name.

He smirks, a glint of excitement in his eyes. "She's fucking *fine,* right?" He rocks back on his heels and gives me a knowing look. Like we're friends or some shit and both in on the same secret.

Until this moment, I had zero issue with Hunt. Thought he was an okay dude with potential, but now... I can't stand the sight of him and I'm two seconds away from punching him in the face, making sure to leave a mark like he left on Kasey.

But I decide to give him a chance and delay punching him right out of the gate by grabbing him by the jersey instead and shoving him against the chain-link fence that surrounds the field.

He brings his arms up in a vain attempt to stop me, but despite the definition he picked up in high school, I have an easy sixty pounds of muscle on him. He's still a kid, and he's not getting away until I'm good and ready to let him go.

"What the fuck, man." His eyes are wide, and I make sure he gets a good look at the fury riding me. "Is she yours or something? Shit, man. She never mentioned having a boyfriend. So if you've got beef, take it up with her." He stops fighting me, both arms raised in surrender. *Idiot.*

"She's seventeen," I snarl, inches from his face.

"What's your point? We're both freshmen. I'm only a year older, probably less than that."

I shake him before slamming him against the fence harder. I can feel the eyes of the team on me, but no one interferes. The only people dumb enough to try are Roman and Emilio, and I made sure both were occupied in the locker room before tracking Deacon down, and that shit took some maneuvering.

"She's a fucking minor," I seethe.

"Bro, lay off. It's not illegal or anything. How do you even know her?"

Shouting comes from the other side of the field. Fuck. I thought I'd have more time, but I guess I'll have to make do with what I have.

"Whatever you think is going on between you two, it ends now. When you see her in class you're going to pretend like you don't even see her."

His jaw tightens, and I know he wants to smart off, but he manages to keep his mouth shut. Only the flaring of his nostrils betrays his emotions. Maybe he isn't that stupid after all.

I drop my hold on him and turn, shouldering past the guys on the team stupid enough to have inched their way closer. Fucking gossips.

"Dom—" Roman calls out, but I shake my head. I'm good. Shit is over. Or at least it should be, but then Deacon goes and opens his fucking mouth.

"I'm not passing on her," he shouts. "If you had your shot and missed it, that's on you. But I'm not gonna look past a fine as fuck piece of ass for your benefit. Not until I've sampled her, at least. When I'm done, I might consider sharing if you still want a taste." He laughs like he's some arrogant frat kid.

My head turns almost as if in slow motion. Everything around me falls away, and all I see is the dipshit in front of me, the three meters between us, and the time it will take me to reach him so I can lay his punk ass out.

"Am I right, boys?" Deacon smirks as he looks around him, meeting the eyes of our teammates. No one responds to him and I watch in satisfaction as his smile slips, and then, I'm on him. I have my left hand on his throat, the right clenched into a tight fist and I draw my arm back.

Right as I move to swing, a hand wraps around my fist, barely managing to stop my momentum. I jerk my gaze to my right only to find Roman holding onto me. Emilio not two steps behind him.

"Your hands," he bites out.

With my left hand still holding Deacon in place, I shake my best friend off. "Fuck my hands." Whatever damage they might sustain will be worth it, only Roman doesn't seem to agree.

"You have a fucked-up shoulder and now you wanna fuck your future just to punch this asshole in the face? Come on, Dom, be smart."

With my eyes locked on his, I ignore Deacon's failed attempts at escape. His hands swing out in a bid to hit me first, save face in front of the team, but my reach is longer than his and all he manages to hit is air. He realizes that he'll never reach me and starts pounding his fist into my left arm.

I grunt, but don't let go.

"Don't be stupid. You're better than this. Don't throw away the season just to punch some punk ass kid."

"Fuck you," Deacon wheezes, not liking Roman's names for him. Personally, I like punk ass more than asshole. It fits him.

My arm is numb. He tagged me on my funny bone and the nerve is spasming, but I'm not about to let up.

Without looking at him, I tighten my grip on his neck.

"My hands will be fine," I snap. "And if they're not, fuck it. It'll be worth it to teach this motherfucker a lesson."

Emilio appears on my other side and both he and Roman work together to shove me back.

I drag Deacon backward with me.

"Dude, let go," Emilio shouts.

"No."

"God dammit," Roman snaps. "For once, will you fucking listen? He isn't worth it."

My nostrils flare. "You have no idea what—"

Emilio curses. "Dammit, Dominique. He's turning blue. Shit. I didn't know black could turn that shade of blue."

I turn to Deacon, eyes narrowing. "Idiot. He's not turning blue. He's turning white. See, around his mouth is muted and almost ashy."

Emilio leans in for a closer look and I use my free hand to smack him upside the head.

"Fucker," he complains, rubbing the back of his head.

"I think you should see a doctor if you think that is blue. Are you color blind?"

Deacon is still struggling, but the strength has been leached out of him and his swings are more like pats on the arm now.

"Not fucking helping," Roman bites out.

"Right." Emilio gives me his best impression of a serious look. "Drop him, man."

I quirk a brow. "That the best you got?"

"What the hell are you all standing around for? Get to moving." Coach shouts, but his voice is far away which means he hasn't caught sight of Deacon yet.

"Fuck." That was Emilio.

"*Hijo de puta.*" And that would be Roman. I've heard *cabrón* out of his mouth enough times to know it basically translates to fucker or smartass, but this one is new.

"What was that?"

"Son of a bitch," Emilio supplies before adding on a groan, "We are so fucked."

I glare at Deacon, seeing the fearful panic in his eyes. I sigh and let go. He slumps to the ground, gasping for breath while clawing at his throat. Coach is about halfway across the field, so we have maybe another minute before this becomes an issue. Enough time for Deacon to get his pussy ass off the ground and fall into line.

I crouch down in front of him, balancing on the balls of my feet, and drop a heavy hand on his shoulder. He's coughing and wheezing, but still manages to look my way, letting me know he's aware of the very real threat I still pose. "You think my issue is that I'm jealous of a punk like you? I'm not. My problem with you is that you left a bruise on Kasey's arm and when I told you to stay the fuck away from her, you mouthed off."

"What the fuck?" Emilio starts, but I block him out.

I'm going to get my point across to this asshole one way or the other. Kasey is off limits, and if he ever lays a hand on her again, I'll fucking kill him.

I grab his chin with a near bruising grip and force him to look up, his back arching from the ground, but he's too weak to fight me. "After today. You're going to pretend you don't know her. You won't look at her. You won't talk to her and you sure as fuck will not touch her. Do you understand?"

He gives a slight nod.

"Good." I release him and stand. "Because the next time I come for you, it won't be anywhere with witnesses."

I stalk toward the field, planning to intercept Coach, when I hear Emilio shout, *"Puta madre, Que te Folle un Pez!"* and turn just in time to see him slam his fist into Deacon's face while he's still on the ground. He knocks him out cold with the single hit.

"What the fuck did that mean?" I ask Roman, a smile curling my lips.

He smirks and tilts his head to the side, thinking. "The literal translation?"

I nod.

"Motherfucker, I hope you get fucked by a fish."

I choke on a laugh. "What? Why a fish?"

He shrugs as Emilio—worked up and chest heaving like he just ran drills—joins us.

"It's harsher in Spanish," Roman adds.

Emilio glares at us both, anger clouding his eyes. "You better start explaining what you meant about him leaving a bruise on Baby Henderson."

Roman's eyes narrow, a vicious glint in his eyes as he takes a step toward Deacon, who is still prone on the ground. I grab his jersey and shake my head. "Not now," I grunt, knowing exactly what he's thinking and agreeing. One hit isn't enough to satisfy any of our need for retribution, which is why he never should have gotten in my way.

His mouth tightens, but he concedes. Then, loud enough for a few of our teammates to hear he says. "Any man weak enough to leave a mark on a woman isn't a man at all. Hunt is going to learn real fucking fast we won't tolerate abusive assholes on this team."

A few of the guys nod their heads, gazes sharpening with that information. Lines are being drawn in the sand as we speak, and I for one can't wait for Deacon to get his next dose of fuck-you medicine.

10

Kasey

I ignore the sounds of partying going on in other parts of the house and focus on my textbook. I've done a pretty good job of hiding from my housemates. I probably shouldn't. My mom keeps sending me messages and leaving voicemails asking if I've made any new friends yet. Kind of hard to do when you're actively avoiding everyone.

But there's this strange irrational part of me that thinks if people see me, they'll know.

They'll know that three days ago Dominique Price dry humped me against a wall before baring my ass in an empty classroom and spanking me. And worse, they'll know I liked it.

I groan miserably into my hands. There has to be something wrong with me when that thought alone has me clenching my thighs and aching for something else to be between them.

My bedroom door swings open. "Kasey!" A female voice singsongs, startling me. "Why are you studying right now when you should be hanging out with me!"

Quinn skips into my room wearing a bright orange bikini top and a pair of cut-off denim shorts. She plops down on my bed beside me, an exaggerated pout on her face.

"You're drunk," I tell her.

She rolls her eyes and lets out a huff. "Obviously. And you should be, too." Then with a whine she adds, "I'm sorry."

I frown at her over the edge of my book. "What is there to be sorry for?"

"I'm your big sister. I'm supposed to make your Kappa Mu experience epic, and instead of having fun with us you're holed up in your room doing homework." She throws herself back on my bed dramatically. "I've failed you."

I roll my eyes. Drunk Quinn is an interesting sight to behold. "You have not failed me," I tell her. "You're a great big."

She perks up. "I am?"

I shrug. Why not? It's not like I have anything to compare her to, and I didn't really come here with any expectations. She's answered any questions I've had and she hasn't been a jerk like some of the other girls in the house, so I'd say we were off to a good start.

"Yep. The best." I turn back to my book, hoping that'll be that and she'll see herself to the door.

"Great. Then as your amazing big sister, I demand you party!" She cheers as she jumps from the bed with a fresh wave of energy. "We need drinks!"

"I'm supposed to study," I tell her, resisting her efforts to drag me from my bed.

"You can study later. You need to have fun!"

"I also need to pass my classes," I remind her, but she doesn't seem worried.

"You will. You're smart. So come on. There's no time like the present."

"Fine," I sigh, and let her drag me from my room. After today's nightmare of an English exam that I am eighty percent sure I completely bombed, I guess I can take a short break and hang out for a little bit. Besides, it doesn't look like she's going to take no for an answer.

Quinn pulls me down the hall and through the main part of the house before pausing right as we get to the doors leading into the backyard. "Clothes!"

"Uh, what about them?"

She whirls on me. "You need them!" She makes a show of smacking her own forehead. "Come on. You need to change."

Now I'm being dragged back the way we came, but instead of going into my room where, you know, all my clothes are, she pulls me into hers and starts rifling through her closet.

"What are you doing?"

She pulls pieces out left and right, tossing them behind her on the floor after she rejects them. "You do know you're going to have to clean that up, right?" I remind her.

"The guys from Alpha Ze are here."

Yippee, stupid drunk frat boys. I am so excited. Cue the sarcasm.

"So. Your point?"

She turns and scowls at me, waving what looks like a purple crop top in my face. "So? So, you're wearing that?"

"What's wrong with what I'm wearing?" I ask, looking down at my jean shorts and oversized crew neck t-shirt.

"Are you modest?" she asks, ignoring my question and going back to sifting through her clothes.

"Not particularly. Why?"

"Because you're always covered up. You're in college. This is where you go to see others and be seen."

I open my mouth to tell her I don't have any desire to be seen when she waves a piece of black fabric in the air. "Found it!" She jumps up and down twice. Like she just won a carnival prize. "Okay, here. Get naked and put this on."

She tosses it to me and I catch the black, silky material. "A swimsuit?" I toss it back to her. "I don't want to go swimming."

She throws it at me again. "You don't wear a swimsuit to go swimming, silly. You wear it so you have an excuse to walk around half naked. Now, hurry up and try it on. You can use my bathroom."

I snort, because my room, which is right next door, is so far away.

Quinn gives me her best shot at an *I'm waiting* look, and I decide to humor her. She's basically the closest thing to a friend I have here and pissing her off probably won't do me any favors.

In the bathroom, I strip out of my clothes and hold the swimsuit out in front of me. It's a one piece, so that's good at least. I wasn't lying when I said I wasn't particularly modest, but I'm not a let it all hang out type of girl either. There are what look to be a dozen little ties and crisscross straps, and I'm not exactly sure how to put the damn thing on.

"Are you decent?" Quinn calls, knocking on the door.

"No!" I tell her, one leg in a hole I'm not entirely sure is meant for my leg.

"Too bad, I'm coming in." And she does. When she sees me, naked and jumping on one foot as I try to get my leg out of the weird knot thingy, she covers her mouth and laughs, eyes wide and shoulders shaking.

"I'm still naked!" I say, crossing one arm over my chest and dropping a hand over the apex of my thighs.

"I can see that." She's laughing so hard, her eyes are watering. "Need a little... help?" she waves at me and I huff out a breath.

"Obviously, yes. I don't know how the heck to get into this."

She giggles and moves closer, helping me untangle my foot as I cover up the goods.

"Here, step in through this one." She helps me slip my feet into the right holes. Why are there so many? And then turns her back so I can shimmy into the thing.

The more on it goes, the less it actually covers, if you can believe that. "Okay I'm turning back around," she calls and then helps me find the holes to slip my arms through.

She gives me a critical once over, pulling the fabric here, tightening it there, before stepping back to examine her work. "You look fucking hot!" she says, a gleam in her eye.

I look down for a second before squeezing my eyes closed. "Are you sure you didn't give me lingerie?" I ask, because wow. And I don't mean that in a good way. Quinn grabs my shoulders and turns me to face the mirror. I open one eye and gasp.

"Holy fu—"

"I know. Right?" She grins. "This one used to be my favorite but since I got these done," she points at her chest, "it doesn't fit anymore. It looks great on you though, so you can keep it."

Keep it? I'm not sure it's even legal to wear. Not in public at least. What I thought was a sleek black one piece is really lingerie pretending to be a swimsuit. The front has a plunging neckline that goes down past my navel, exposing the top of my crotch—thank god I got waxed last week. Holding the two sides in place is a series of crisscross ties that lace up the entire front until they reach my neck where they tie like a halter top in the back. The material over my boobs barely covers my nipples, so I have an insane amount of cleavage, and the back is virtually non-existent. My entire back is on display and half my ass hangs out of the teeny tiny bottoms, giving me a persistent wedgie.

"Stop adjusting everything," Quinn chides, smacking my hand away as she tugs my bottoms up, not down, exposing even more of my ass. "It's supposed to be like this."

I gawk at her. "I'm almost naked. Actually, I think this is more provocative than being naked."

Her smile is wide. "I know, right? Now let's go get wasted! It's Friday night and you've been here a week already. It's time to let loose."

Before I can object, she is literally dragging me out of the bathroom. "Quinn. Stop."

Does she? Of course not. And who would have guessed that my five-foot-four sorority sister was this strong. We're back at the door and not giving me any time to prepare myself, she swings it wide open and shouts, "Time for Jell-O shots, bitches!"

The girls outside laugh and cheer, and then with all the confidence in the world, Quinn heads for the table where said Jell-O shots are lined up in a rainbow of colors. Several of my sorority sisters move to follow her, everyone barely dressed in a multitude of swim attire.

I get a few heated stares from some of the guys and ignore them as I head for an empty chair by the pool where I spot some sunscreen. I'm blond-haired, blue-eyed, and so white that my friend Monique jokes that instead of tanning, I turn translucent.

A joke, obviously, but she isn't far off. I was cursed with zero melanin, so the sun and I have never exactly been friends. Growing up in the summer I would tell Aaron he was born selfish since he stole it all from our mom before I even had a chance. So unfair. A few hours outdoors and he turns a golden color that makes him look like a modern-day Apollo. Meanwhile, I go from white to pink to red in a matter of minutes if I don't slather myself at least in SPF80.

After squirting some sunscreen in my hands, I massage it into my arms and legs when a shadow falls over me, blocking out some of the harsh rays from the sun.

"Want me to get your back?" A masculine voice asks, and I turn to find Deacon behind me, beer in hand and a hesitant smile on his face.

"Oh, hey. What are you doing here?" I ask, and lift a hand over my eyes to see him better. He's wearing black swim shorts and no shirt, and has on mirrored sunglasses so I can't make out his eyes.

"I'm in Alpha Ze," he tells me.

"Ah, it all makes sense now."

He tilts his head to the side.

"What does?"

"That cocky charismatic charm of yours that you're able to flip on and off whenever you like. Nice chatting this week, by the way. Coffee was great," I tell him and he grimaces. After we ran into each other I thought, I don't know, that we'd actually try the whole friend thing, but I guess when he realized he'd be stuck in the friend zone he didn't want to waste his time.

We never talked after that day and in class he wouldn't even look at me. If he wanted me to get the hint, I heard him loud and clear. I just wish he wasn't such an asshole about it. I don't understand why guys can't just be friends with a girl. Why does it always have to be something else?

"About that," he rubs the back of his neck and is silent for a beat before dropping down on the lounge beside me.

11

Kasey

Deacon massages his throat and I get the feeling he's working his way up to telling me something I'm not going to like to hear. When the seconds turn into minutes, I shift my focus back to applying my sunscreen. Seriously, if I don't, I will fry.

"I didn't mean to ghost you."

I put a little lotion on two fingers and massage it through the crisscross ties running down the front of the suit. I look ridiculous doing it but a girl has to do what a girl has to do.

"So why did you?" I ask. My feelings aren't hurt by it, to be honest. I have plenty of friends and I'm not actively searching for more. I guess I mostly just find it annoying. I don't get why guys only see value in women if there's a chance of them getting laid. It's bullshit if you ask me.

"Look, I don't want to cause drama and shit."

I wait. I don't know what he's looking for from me, but I'm not going to help him out here. He approached me, so if this is going to be an issue—him talking to me—he's just as welcome to walk away.

"A few of the guys on the team aren't cool with the idea of us hanging out," he tells me and I stiffen. Dammit. Because, of course, Dominique didn't forget about the bruise after he left the classroom. I mean, he had no problem forgetting, but not Deacon. Not when it gave him the opportunity to be an even bigger asshole.

I grind my teeth together and ask, "Was it all three of them?" If it was, then I have three Devils to get back at instead of just the one.

Deacon shakes his head, "I don't think so." He pauses. "Not in the beginning at least. I think only my QB had a problem with it, but those three are tight—"

"Yeah," I sigh. "I know."

We're both quiet for a moment.

"He your ex or something?" Deacon asks.

I snort. "Definitely not. We've never dated and trust me when I say, we never will."

One dark brow raises over the rim of his glasses. "You sure about that? The way Price was acting, it's the way a jealous ex would be if he caught someone sniffing around his girl."

My lip curls. "First, I'm not a dog. No one is sniffing anywhere. And second, yes, I'm sure about that. I've known him since we were kids. We're all sort of in the same friend group and he's roommates with my older brother. He takes the term 'overprotective' to the extreme." They all do. They're the bonus brothers I never asked for. Well, except for Dominique. I mean, I still didn't ask for him. That part is true. But of all the guys, he is the one I most definitely do not see as a brother. Even more so after what happened between us earlier this week.

Asshole.

Deacon nods, and I hate that I still can't see his eyes, so I decide to do something about it. Reaching up, I pluck the shades off his face, folding them down and setting them beside me.

"So, what did those three knuckleheads do, exactly? I'm assuming threats were involved, or did he go on a power trip and threaten to have you removed from the team?"

A flash of fear appears on his face, but it's gone a second later. Shit. Dominique really got to him.

"No. Not that. I'm still on the team." His Adam's apple bobs as he visibly swallows. "He can't get me kicked off, anyway."

I inwardly groan. Why are the pretty ones so dumb? Dominique could absolutely get Deacon removed from the team. All it would take is one phone call to his parents, a sizable donation, and boom. Goodbye, Suncrest U. Hello, community college.

I decide not to tell him that because he seems a little freaked out as it is. If you didn't grow up in Sun Valley, then it's safe to assume you don't know how big of a deal Dominique's family is. Deacon probably knows who the Prices are, the same way everyone in the U.S. knows who Bill Gates is. But, if you saw him walking down the street, you'd probably walk past him none the wiser, and it's not like you'd know who his kids were or what they looked like.

"Yo, D!" someone shouts, pulling Deacon's attention. "Is that her? The chick you got your ass kicked for?" He gives me a heated look, biting his fist. "Damn, man. I get it."

"Reed, fuck off," Deacon snarls right as I give the guy a one-fingered salute.

"Come on, man. No need to be like that. I was just complimenting your girl. I'd tap that for sure." He makes a thrusting motion with his hips and Deacon groans, covering his face with his hand.

"I apologize on behalf of my idiot frat brother. You probably won't believe me, but he's actually a pretty cool guy when he's not wasted like he is now."

Yeah. Not so sure about that but I leave it alone.

"He said you got your ass kicked. That was because of me?"

He sighs. "It's nothing. Can we drop it?"

Uh, no. No, we cannot drop it. I told Dominique it was an accident. Obviously he didn't let it go, but I'd expect him to throw his weight around. Maybe threaten Deacon or try to intimidate him somehow. Physically assaulting him is taking it to another level. Why was he so riled up about this?

"I'm going to need a play by play. I can get that from you or from some of your brothers who, by the sounds of it, are in the know. Up to you."

His jaw flexes, but instead of telling me what happened he asks, "Did you lie and tell him I hurt you?"

"Excuse me?"

He turns narrowed eyes my way. "I've gone over what happened in my head a few times and Dominique said I hurt you. Left a bruise but," he shakes his head. "I never hit you. I don't hit women. I'm trying to figure out why you'd tell him otherwise."

His nostrils flare and damn, he looks pissed. All over again, I get the feeling he isn't someone safe. It's like he hides this dangerous edge about him under layers of confidence and charisma.

"Well?" he snaps.

I lift my arm in answer. When he sees the still purple mark, he grabs my arm and tugs it closer, taking me with it since, well, it's sort of attached. I all but fall into his lap, but he doesn't even notice. His eyes lock on my skin. Flexing his fingers, he wraps them around my arm in the exact same spot before cursing and shoving my arm away.

"I didn't tell him you hit me. I didn't even say this came from you." I sit back and tuck my legs beneath me. "He saw us talking when you walked me to the athletics building. Then he saw the bruise. My poker face is pretty awesome. Sorry about that. He asked if it came from you and well ..." I trail off.

"When we collided?" he asks.

I nod.

He sucks on his teeth. "I grabbed you. Harder than I should have. I get why you got all jumpy after that when I tugged on your hand. I," He pauses. "It wasn't on purpose. I mean, leaving that mark. Hurting you." He hangs his head. "I am not that guy. I'm *trying* not to be that guy."

"Have you ever been that guy before?" I ask, needing to know if he's safe. If he's someone I should be careful around.

He shakes his head, and I exhale a relieved breath. "No. My old man was. But I won't ever allow myself to become a monster the way he was." There is steely determination in his voice. "I'm sorry. We're getting into deep shit when we barely know each other." He chuckles, but it's forced.

"It's all good. And thanks. For the apology, I mean."

He nods.

"I still want that play by play, though," I remind him.

I wait. He tips back his beer, his throat working as he takes a long pull.

"Stalling will get you nowhere."

He grunts and then shakes his head. "We had some words. It's over now."

"Hey, Reed?" I call out. I stand and scan the backyard, looking for Deacon's frat brother who brought this all up in the first place.

Deacon hisses. "Kasey, drop it."

"Yo!" Reed hollers.

"I have questions." I nod my head and indicate for him to come over. He says a few more words to the guys he was talking to before slapping one on the back and heading our way.

"Kasey—" There's a warning in Deacon's voice. It's cute. I mean if I don't listen when Dominique gets all growly, why would I listen now?

"You're welcome to tell me yourself," I remind him.

He presses his lips into a firm line. Alrighty then.

As soon as Reed is close I say, "What happened with Deacon and Dominique Price?"

Reed whistles. "Aw, man. That was some rough shit." He ignores the death stare Deacon is giving him and dives into his recount of Tuesday's events. Dominique getting in Deacon's face. Choking him. How Deacon nearly passed out.

Deacon is quiet the entire time, chin down and shoulders slumped.

"And then the other guy, what's his name again?" He snaps his fingers before answering his own question. "E! That's what all the jocks call him. So Dominique is walking away, point made, am I right?" He wiggles his brows. "When his buddy, E, starts talking in Spanish and punches Deacon while he's still on the ground. It was fucking savage."

Deacon groans. "Thanks for the recount, man. Appreciate it."

Reeds misses the sarcasm in Deacon's voice.

"Emilio punched you?" I ask. Now, that surprises me the most.

Deacon sighs. "Yeah. I don't think he or Valdez knew why Dominique was in my face. They were trying to haul him off me at first. Talk him down and shit." His mouth tightens. "After Dominique made his point, he warned me off you and mentioned that," he points his beer toward my arm, "Chavez blew a gasket and clocked me. Now that I see it, can't say I really blame him. I'd be pissed too if someone hurt a girl I cared about."

"I'm sorry. The guys can be overprotective."

"It's all good now. Like I said. It's done."

"Fuck no, it's not. D, you haven't told her about practices, man."

"Shut the fuck up, bro," he grinds out, but Reed is drunk, making him oblivious to Deacon's warning.

"What's going on in practice?"

It's Reed who answers. "Deacon is getting his ass handed to him. All day, every day. Left tackles aren't protecting him. He's getting sacked damn near every play he runs. It's fucking brutal."

My eyes widen. "You're kidding?" Why wasn't his team watching his back? The quarterback was the most vulnerable player on the field. One wrong hit and he could be seriously injured.

"Nope. Price's shoulder is fucked up, right?" Wait, it is? What happened to his shoulder? "So all he's doing in practice is throwing. Him and Valdez run drills while Deacon starts on the field. Five plays in on day one and it dawns on Deacon that protection is bad and it's staying bad. He starts to scramble when he gets the ball. Man doesn't want to get hit."

Deacon is rigid, every muscle in his face drawn tight. He doesn't like hearing this.

"This shit goes on for three days," Reed says, waving three fingers in the air. "And then out of nowhere, Price takes to the field, smacks our boy here upside the head, and tells him, *'You're fast. Play faster. Trust your feet.'* It was solid advice but Deacon isn't having it. He's pissed."

"Can you blame me?" Deacon snaps.

Reed lifts both hands in the air. "Nope. I'd be an asshole, too. Maybe not to the dude's face like that, but," he shrugs. "Anyway, Hunt is mouthing off. He tells Price he's playing dirty, fucking with his protection, and damn, you should have seen the look on Price's face. He told Deacon if he wanted protection, give them someone worth protecting. And if he doesn't like getting hit, then go play fucking tennis."

I wince. Dominique's never been one to mince words. "That was harsh."

"But, effective," Reed smirks.

I turn to Deacon, who's still glaring, but when he sees me looking he nods. "It did the job," he sighs. "Got my head out of my ass and back in the game."

"And made you a damn better quarterback. Deacon learned in three days what takes most quarterbacks years to figure out, and he's not buckling under the pressure. He's playing smart."

"Has Dom backed off? Is your defensive line helping you out, now?"

Deacon snorts. "No. I'm still on Prices' shit list. But now," he shrugs, "I do my part to not get hit."

"So, he's still getting hit a lot." Reed supplies and Deacon shoots him another glare. "Hey, don't get pissy with me, my friend. You're just mad because that asshole made you a better player and you don't like it."

"Yeah, whatever." Deacon finishes his beer and stands. "I need another drink. You?"

"Uh, sure." He nods and I watch as he heads over to the coolers the girls placed near the pool. Once he's out of earshot, I turn back to Reed and ask, "What's he going to do?

Getting sacked in practice is one thing, but he can't be left defenseless in a game. He'll end up seriously hurt."

Reed gives me a sobering look. "I think he's hoping you can help him out with that."

Me? What the hell was I supposed to do?

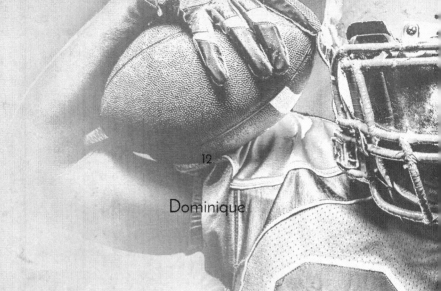

12

Dominique

Aaron's riding the line again. He isn't sleeping and jumping at loud sounds. I know what's coming and I'm trying to head it off, but the asshole standing in front of me isn't making that easy.

"Bro, we had a deal?"

Aaron throws on his leather jacket and swipes his keys off the table, heading for the front door.

"I'm not going to do anything stupid," he assures me, but we both know that's a lie.

"You heard what the doc—"

His jaw clenches. "I'm going to live my life. Okay? Can you get on board with that, man?"

I grind my teeth together. This is a bad idea and he knows it, but I can see by the look in his eyes I don't have a shot in hell of talking him out of it. I never do. Not when he gets like this.

Henderson is a walking, talking stick of dynamite just waiting to explode. When we were kids, he was always a self-destructive shit, but adult Aaron is on a whole 'nother level. We've all got baggage, but the shit Aaron needs to unpack is traumatic as fuck, and I only know the half of it. But we made a deal. I'm not about to let him weasel out of it.

"When you stop being a lying sack of shit, maybe." I shrug and wait to see how he responds. It can go one of two ways. Brotherhood will get the better of him and he'll back down. Nine and a half times out of ten, he's true to his word and he hates being called a liar. Addicts are liars and Aaron refuses to be one of them.

I see the flicker in his eyes. The moment of hesitation at my words and then... *fuck*. There's that other half. The times when he decides not to give a fuck because he's too far up his own ass to think straight.

"Aaron—"

"You know me," he says, and there's a plea in his voice, so I nod. "You know I've been clean. For two years I've stayed clean. No missteps. I've stayed on the fucking wagon, man."

"I know." Which is why what he's doing now is pissing me off. It's like he forgot what the first year was like. The depression. The withdraws. He was so fucking sick back then he had to take a full semester off. And now he wants to risk it all for a party and a piece of ass. I shake my head. This was a mistake.

"It's a pool party. There will be booze, but we both know booze was never my problem."

No. It wasn't. Aaron's issue started as a little recreational weed until he fucked up. Got behind the wheel while high and wrapped his car around a tree, injuring his passengers— Roman, Emilio, and me. Shit got ugly after the accident and we didn't speak for close to a year after that.

What none of us knew at the time though, was that Aaron almost went to juvie for it. He was a minor driving while under the influence and had over forty grams of weed on him when paramedics picked us up. Once released, he was charged with a class C felony. His lawyer couldn't make it go away. Not entirely. But the DA's office offered him a deal and with approval from a judge and his parent's consent, they signed off on him becoming an informant for the Sun Valley P.D.

Big fucking mistake.

Roman's dad was chief back then and made the arrangements. If Roman ever found out, there'd be hell to pay, which is why even after shit was smoothed out between us all, Aaron never mentioned it.

Shit should have been straightforward. On paper, Aaron was supposed to tip the cops off about corner dealers selling to kids at our school, but what really happened was they forced him into the deep end. They had a sixteen-year-old worming his way into the drug world and shit got messy.

I don't know all the details of everything that went down. I know shit escalated with drugs. Weed turned into molly and that turned into coke. There was a girl he refuses to talk about. And a drug deal went south that Aaron got caught up in. He hasn't shared the full story, but on top of the addiction he got a nice case of PTSD. When he's having an episode things get heavy. The way he reacts, you'd think he'd been to war. I guess in a roundabout way he was.

Aaron worked on getting clean before we moved in together and I helped get him out of the CI program as soon as I learned he was in it. Fuckers didn't want to let him go, but I made sure they realized they didn't have a choice. Sometimes it pays to be a Price. This was one of those times.

But the road to recovery is a long one, and staying clean isn't the only thing Aaron needs to worry about. "Access to drugs isn't what I'm worried about. I know you're good." The first year was rough but the last two, he's been solid.

Aaron lets out an exasperated sigh. "I'll be fine."

"You jumped me when I slammed the back door earlier."

He closes his eyes, hands fisted at his sides. "You caught me off guard."

Yeah. I'd been doing that a lot lately. It's why I've made it a point to be around as much as possible. I go to class, the field, and then straight home. I've met up with Aaron for lunch between classes all week, and when he's felt up for it, he kicks it at the field and catches up on his schoolwork while he waits for me to finish.

It's not ideal. We don't do secrets in our crew. But, this ... this is Aaron's damage. It's not my place to tell my boys. Aaron will do that when he's good and ready, so for now, this is what works.

But part of why it works is because we avoid scenes like what Aaron is about to put himself in. Greek parties are loud. Rowdy. People get into stupid shit and no, I don't think Aaron will slip up when it comes to drugs. He worked to fucking hard for his sobriety. But this week he's been off and I'm waiting for the other shoe to drop.

"There's going to be loud music. Probably shit with a heavy bass. People are going to be shouting. People are going to rub against you when you walk by. How do you think you'll react?" I'm not his dad. I'm not going to order him around, but he needs to see this for what it is. A bad idea.

"I'm going. You wanna babysit, be my guest, but I'm climbing the walls here, Dom." He slams a palm to his chest. "I can't breathe and I know I'm fucked up in the head right now, but this is what I've come up with and I'm seeing it through."

I grab my phone and slide it into my back pocket. "Let's go, then."

Aaron's shoulders relax and we head out. He tells me on the way that the party we're headed to is at Kappa Mu. Kasey's sorority house. *Shit.*

We haven't talked since the classroom. I'm a dick. She knows that already. This isn't some new revelation. But I took shit too far that day. And if Aaron finds out what I did to his baby sister, what I still think about doing to her, I'm fucked.

"I see you're having fun," Quinn says, a smirk on her face as she moves to stand up beside me. "Any chance your hottie has a brother?"

I follow her eyes and see that she's ogling Deacon. "Not that I know of, but he's not my hottie. We just happen to have English together this semester so, you should go for it."

Her eyes bug out and she whips toward me. "Seriously? You wouldn't mind?"

I laugh. "Nope. He's all yours. Deacon isn't really my type."

She looks at me like I just spoke a foreign language. "Have you seen the guy?" she asks. "That fine specimen of a man right there is everyone's type."

"He's good-looking, I'll give you that. But—"

"But? There are no buts." She places the back of her hand against my forehead. Then my cheeks. "Are you feeling okay?

No fever, but I'm worried about you. Maybe you should lie down. All this sun is getting to you."

I smack her hand away. "I'm fine," I tell her with an exasperated breath. "I just don't do players. He's nice, but he's on the football team and he's a Greek. Pass."

"You do realize you're a Greek right?"

I shrug. "So, I'm a hypocrite. Sue me. Are you really going to stand here and continue trying to convince me to go for him, or are you going to take your fine ass over there before one of our sisters shoots their shot?"

"Oh, my God, you're right." Quinn fluffs her hair and adjusts her boobs. Yes, she actually shifted her girls around before glancing at me with an expectant look. "How do I look?"

"Hot! Go get him."

She gives an excited squeal before taking a deep breath and marching toward him. Deacon drifted back to his friend group a little while ago, giving me a much-needed respite after everything he and Reed had unloaded. A part of me wants to help. I feel a little responsible for what he's going through, but a bigger part of me really doesn't want to get involved. I don't want an excuse to seek Dominique out. If I do ... I don't know. But it isn't going to be good. I'm angry and a little hurt, though mostly angry. This is the second time something like this has happened between us and both times he ghosts me.

What the hell is his problem? I'm not asking for a relationship or even a repeat event. All I'm asking for is some human decency. It's really not too much to ask.

But, whatever. This is Dominique I'm talking about here. I turn and grab a water bottle from one of the coolers and head for the pool. There's a pink sprinkle, donut-shaped floaty with my name on it.

One of the Alpha Ze guys helps me maneuver my way onto it without jumping into the pool because not gonna lie, that water is cold.

I'm laying back, enjoying the music and chatter around me when something in the air shifts. I don't know how else to describe it. Sunglasses firmly in place, I turn my head to the side just in time to see my brother and—would you look at that—Dominique, arrive.

For a second, a flash of panic hits me square in the chest and I look down at myself. Fuck. I'm dead. So dead. When Dominique sees what I'm—hold on. I cut that thought off and scoff. What am I even thinking? Fuck what Dominique thinks. Quinn was right. I look hot. No way in hell am I going to let that asshole shame me for wearing this suit. I'm going to own it.

I track their progress through the yard, grateful no one can see my eyes because I'm totally staring. Aaron, being the friendly guy he is, dives right in on the fun and joins a few of the guys at one of the backyard games the girls must have set up. The one where you toss hacky sacks at an angled board and try to get it through the hole.

"Hey, what's that game called?" I ask one of the guys swimming next to me. I'm not sure what his name is. He hooks his arms over the side of my floaty and looks to where I'm pointing. "Corn hole," he tells me, and then instead of swimming away, which was what I'd been hoping for, his eyes do a slow and obvious perusal of my body. "I'm Ignacio, but everyone calls me Iggy."

"Hey. I'm—"

"Kasey!" A familiar voice barks out my name. Well, that took longer than expected. *Not.*

I turn my head to find Dominique, arms folded over his chest and dark eyes ablaze. He's not wearing sunglasses like virtually everyone else here, so I can spot his glare from the edge of the pool and offer him a little wave. His nostrils flare.

Dressed in black jogger pants that taper at the ankle and a white crew t-shirt that hugs his broad shoulders and impressive chest, I have to fight the urge not to lick my lips. Has he always looked this good? Who am I kidding? Yes.

He's wearing his usual red Beast Mode sneakers, but he's changed his hair. For as long as I've known him, Dominique's kept it braided back over his scalp. Sometimes they're thick braids. Other times they're thin. But for the first time, there are no braids. Sometime this week he got his hair cut and damn, it looks good on him.

A line up and fade make his features appear sharper, and he's added a razor part design. Two parallel lines that start at his temple and slant up enough to form a peak before curving down and back. Almost like a lightning bolt.

"I didn't think this was really your scene." I keep my tone casual, my expression carefree. I know people are watching, the girls already trying to figure out how we know one another. This is exactly why I didn't want him and the other guys here when I moved in. They draw too much attention.

"Get out of the pool." His voice is hard.

"Pass. I'm enjoying it here."

I swear steam comes out of his ears.

"Kasey—" There's a warning there. One I should probably listen to, but where is the fun in that?

"Dominique," I retort.

His jaw is tight, a vein bulging in his neck. This is too good. Alpha Ze guy—what was his name again? Oh, right, Iggy—is still clinging to my floaty, but his eyes keep bouncing back and forth from me to Dom and then back again.

"Hey," I draw his attention.

He turns, expression a little nervous. Well, shit. That won't work. I turn my smile up a notch and shift to my side which gives him a better view of my breasts. "Sorry. He's so rude. I'm Kasey." I pick up where we left off, suddenly interested in chatting with the guy.

He swallows hard, eyes locked on my chest.

"So, what year are you?" I ask, and right as I'm about to trail a finger over his arm Dominique snaps, "Rojas. Off limits. Get your ass away from her."

Iggy jumps back as if he's been electrocuted and makes quick work of following Dom's orders. "Yeah, man. Of course. I was just, uh, making conversation. You know?"

Dominique doesn't answer him. He gives Iggy a flat stare before dismissing him with a look and turning his attention back to me. "I won't ask again, Kasey."

I flip him off. There are a few muffled laughs from the yard, and I spot Deacon and Reed barely keeping themselves in check. Dominique sees them too. *Oh, shit.* He stalks in their direction. *Shit. Shit.*

Deacon sees him coming and squares his shoulders, nostrils flaring. Double shit. He's not going to back down. "Dom!" I paddle my arms to reach the pool's edge but wind up spinning myself in circles. Navigation on a giant donut is not as easy as it might seem, but one of the guys is nice enough to give me a push to the shallow end and then I'm off. I jump in the thigh deep water. Gah! Cold. And hop up the steps.

Dominique is in Deacon's face. No clue what he's saying, but it doesn't look like they're discussing the weather. Everyone is watching. Waiting for fists to fly, but yeah, no. Not happening.

I shove myself between the guys and push Dominique in the chest as hard as I can. He moves back a few steps, but only because he was willing to.

"Happy now? I'm out." He's glaring over my shoulder, still not looking at me. I turn and clear my throat to get Deacon's attention. His eyes shift and he looks down, and then all of a sudden I'm shoved back behind Dominique and he's all growly, saying, "Don't fucking look at her."

Then he's tearing his shirt off his head and shoving it down over mine. When my head pops out he helps me get my arms through the sleeves, and then he's back to shoving me behind him again. Whoa. He's seriously losing it right now. I've never seen him like this.

"I thought I made myself clear," he says, voice dipped low and threatening.

"What is your problem, man? She's not your girl. Back the fuck off."

Okay, so true, I am most definitely not his girl, but still, even I know that was the wrong thing to say. *Idiot.* It's like he *wants* to get his ass kicked again. The muscles of Dominique's back tighten, and wow, is it a good-looking back. Why have I never seen his bare back like this before?

More heated words are exchanged, but I'm not really paying attention, too intent on tracing the lines between his shoulders and down his back with my gaze. That accomplished, I reach out and begin physically tracing the lines with my finger.

He stiffens. I don't let that deter me. I follow the path, applying light pressure, and some of the tension falls away. His muscles flex and Dominique takes a deep breath, no longer talking.

When I reach the dip at the base of his spine I lean forward, resting my head against him. A tremor rolls through him. I can feel the twist of his muscles. He peers over his shoulder, but I'm not looking at him so I don't know what he's thinking. I should move away. Stop touching him. *Why am I touching him?*

That thought gets me out of my head and I jerk back, but he's there. He turns, grabs my still raised hand, and pulls me to him. Not in an embrace or anything like that. Dominique doesn't do public affection. Not that he's ever been affectionate with me. No. We fight. I guess we also sometimes angry kiss and dry hump, but whether that was a one off or will be a repeat event is yet to be decided.

So no, no embrace. But I'm right beside him. The heat from his bare skin seeping into me.

"What are you doing?" he asks. I meet his dark-brown stare. He doesn't look mad, at least not right at this moment. He looks ... confused.

"Are you done?"

His brows pull together. "Am I done with what?"

"Being an asshole."

I open my mouth to add that he needs to stop laying into Deacon over nothing, but catch myself. He's calming down. I'd be stupid to say something I know will just piss him off again.

"You wanted me out of the pool. I'm out. Okay? Can we just … I don't know, go inside? Cool down for a bit?"

He works his jaw, but nods. Relief sweeps through me. Good. "Come on, then." I'm waiting to see if he's going to follow before heading for the door when I catch sight of my brother right as he's turning.

He sees me. Smiles. Waves. When he sees what I'm wearing, a wrinkle forms between his brows.

"What are you—" He eyes the shirt I'm wearing and then spots a shirtless Dominique behind me. "Why are you wearing his shirt?" There's genuine confusion in his voice and my heart starts to race because shit, um … I go with the first thing that pops in my head.

"Because Dominique is an asshole." Yep. True and relevant. Score one for me.

"Huh?" Why does he sound confused? It's not like this is a new revelation.

I decide to elaborate. "He's a dick and made me put this on because my swimsuit is *indecent*." I make air quotes and glare at Dominique for exaggerated effect. "Did you tell him to cock block me?" I add, turning my glare on my brother. "Because that shit is not cool, Aaron. I know you guys are roommates and all, but I don't need babysitters at my own house."

His eyes widen and he gets this look on his face that screams *abort. Abort.*

I love my brother, but he's never really been one for confrontation. Not with me, at least. I happen to have a bit of a mean streak and a solid record for always getting revenge. What I just said basically implies I'll cock block him the rest of the year if he tries to cock block me. I should feel bad. The panic written all over his face is just too good.

"I wouldn't do that. I—" he sputters, and I fold my arm over my chest, lifting a single brow.

"Bullshit. You absolutely would."

He huffs and then seems to rally himself, which surprises me.

"Was it?"

"Was it what?"

"Indecent. Was the swimsuit indecent?" No. Maybe. Okay, yeah, I mean, have you seen it? It was a lot. But I wasn't going to admit that to my brother.

"It's a swimsuit." I argue. "Top. Bottom. The usual."

"Kasey—" He's glaring. At me. What the hell?

"What is going on right now. This is not how this," I wave at the space between us, "works. Dominique is an asshole. I yell at you and you apologize for him being an asshole. That's how this works."

He just stares for a beat and says, "Fine, let's see it. If he's wrong, I'll apologize for him being an asshole."

My eyes widen. "What? No!"

He gives me an are-you-serious expression. "It's a swimsuit. I've seen you in a swimsuit."

Dominique is shaking beside me fighting not to laugh. I push him. "This is your fault."

He smirks. "Show him the suit, Baby Henderson."

I grind my teeth together. Fine. I'm not embarrassed. I fucking rocked this swimsuit. With my eyes on his, I tug the t-shirt off. Dominique's eyes stay trained on my face, but I don't miss the hitch in his breath.

There's a gasp. "Jesus Christ." That was from Aaron. "Don't look at my little sister like that, you fucking perv." That catches both our attention, but when I look, Aaron isn't talking to Dominique, he's glowering at the guys he's been playing corn hole with. "She's only se—"

"Hey!"

He turns.

"Don't you dare," I warn. If he tells everyone I'm seventeen I will murder him. He must see that in my eyes, because he manages to keep his mouth shut and gives Dominique some weird look. Silent communication passes between them, and then the shirt is being shoved back over my head, only this time when my head pops out it's to see Aaron heading for the door.

I follow him, Dominique right behind me, and as soon as we're all safely inside Aaron whirls on me. "What the fuck were you thinking? Do you know what goes through those guys' heads when they look at you? Shit."

I wait. I'm not really sure what is happening right now. Aaron has always been protective, but he's also always let me do my thing. This is different. Almost like he's spiraling. I don't think all this anger is really about me. At least I hope it isn't.

"It's a swimsuit. I'm at a party in my own house I might add. I don't care how guys look at me or what goes on in their head. As long as they don't touch me without permission, I'm good. You're overreacting—"

"Overreacting? Overreacting! Jesus Christ." He spears his fingers through his shaggy blond hair.

"You said that already."

"Well, it warranted a repeat."

I smile a little at that. He takes a few deep breaths and then turns to Dominique and gives him a fist bump. "Thanks, man. I appreciate you looking out."

Dominique grunts and meets my stare. There's a warning, as if he's saying *don't you dare say a thing about what happened in the classroom.*

I glare back, my eyes conveying my own response. *I'm not an idiot, asshole.*

"I'm gonna go down to the park. I need to get the image of my baby sister in that," he nods in my direction, "out of my head. I can drop—"

"I'm good. Go ahead. Kasey can give me a lift."

I scowl, but Aaron's not paying attention. "Cool man. I'll see you later back at the house."

He heads for the door, but at the last second Dominique stops him. "Yo!"

He waits until Aaron turns to face him. "If something comes up, you call. You hear me?"

More silent communication passes between them, and damn, is that sort of creepy. I know Aaron and Dominique are friends. Best friends now. But it's like they have their own language, and there is seriously something going on with my brother that definitely has nothing to do with my swimsuit.

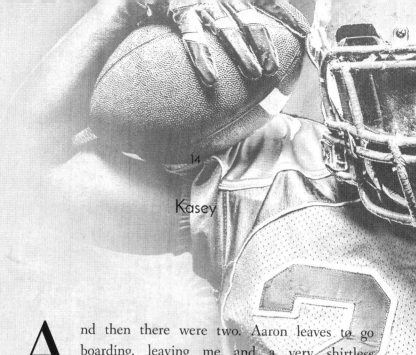

14

Kasey

And then there were two. Aaron leaves to go boarding, leaving me and a very shirtless Dominique behind. Right. Clothes. He needed clothes. Which meant I needed clothes. Gah.

I head for my bedroom, conscious of Dominique's silent steps behind me. Once inside, I head for my dresser and pull out a pair of yoga pants and a sweater. I look down at the shirt. I don't want to give it back. It's soft and comfy and it smells like him. Like cinnamon and sandalwood and yum. *Oh my god.* I cannot believe I thought that. Not keeping the shirt. I am not that girl and no, I am not hung up on him. Just no. He's an asshole. An inconsiderate, domineering jerkface.

I pull it over my head and hold it out to Dominique, who's just standing there. Staring. It's the first time I've gotten a good look at his front and yeah, it's just as good as the back. Better actually, which is completely unfair.

His chest is wide, sculpted. He has abs that should be illegal. And those lines ... you know the ones.

I want to trail my fingers over those lines, lick his hip bone, stroke his abs. Wait. No. Fuck. I do not want to do any of those things. *Come on, Kasey, get it together.*

Alright then. I am not keeping the shirt and he really needs to put it on and leave. I cannot be around him right now. I think the sun addled my brain or something.

"Take it," I say, and give the shirt in question a little shake.

He's not looking at the shirt though. He's looking at me. And the look in his eyes isn't an innocent one. It's the same look he gave me in the classroom. Heated. Hungry. *Fuck.* I drop the shirt.

"Christ." He runs a hand over his head. "That thing is fucking indecent."

I look down at myself and yeah, he's not wrong, but neither was Quinn. I'm glad she offered me the swimsuit. Once I got over the shock of the thing, I decided I liked it. I don't care what anyone else thinks.

I've never had a hard time getting a guy's attention, present company not included, but I'm attractive in a cute sort of way. Not beautiful. Not hot or sexy. Just, cute. I have round cheeks, curly blond hair, bright blue eyes and one of those faces that people look at and think to themselves, *she's cute.*

This swimsuit takes me from cute to sexy and I'm not going to lie, I like it. I like feeling sexy, and as much as I hate to admit it, I like the way Dominique is looking at me while I'm in it. Which, yes, I know that's bad. It's the sun. Totally blaming the sun for my crazy stupid thoughts right now because I shouldn't like the way he's looking at me. In fact, I should be snapping at him for it. But I'm not. I need to steer us back onto safe ground.

"Thanks for the unsolicited opinion," I tell him.

"Put that back on." He nods to the shirt.

"Pass. I don't take orders from assholes."

His eyes narrow. "Put on the shirt."

"No. In case you didn't notice, Kappa Mu is having a party. One I plan on getting back to and enjoying. You should have left with Aaron, but since you didn't, I'll be nice and let you borrow my car. But I'm going to go have fun." I'd breeze past him out the door if he wasn't still blocking it, but because he is, I lean back against my dresser and fold my arms over my chest to wait.

His jaw tics.

"Put on the shirt, Kasey."

"No."

"Dammit. Put on the fucking shirt."

"Make me, asshole."

Okay, that last comment, probably not a great choice of words. Dominique closes the distance between us. Capturing my hips in his hands, he jerks me to him.

"Why do you always have to fight me on shit?"

I give him an incredulous look. "You're kidding, right?"

His nostrils flare.

"You do not get to dictate what I wear or do or anything about my life. You don't own me. Get that through your head." Something in me snaps. All my frustration from before, my anger and hurt at his dismissal comes rushing to the surface. Where does he get off? "You think that, what, since we fooled around in a classroom that you all of a sudden get to make demands? That's not how this works, Dom!" I shove at his chest. "Get the hell out of my way."

He shifts his stance, still blocking me.

"Dominique—"

"Put on the shirt or take off that suit. You're not going out where all those fraternity punks are in that."

I bite the inside of my cheek until I taste blood. "Fine," I snap.

Surprise flashes in his eyes and he takes a step back, giving me some space, but I'm not going to put on his stupid cinnamon smelling shirt. Since he wants me to take off the swimsuit, I'll take it off.

I grab the straps of the swimsuit and tug them down, pulling my arms out.

"What are you doing?"

Ignoring him, I push the swimsuit down past my ribcage, exposing my breasts.

"Jesus Christ!"

A small smile curls my lip and I shove the swimsuit down over my hips, letting it pool at my feet. I swallow hard, but refuse to be embarrassed as I raise my eyes to his. "Happy now?" My voice is surprisingly even, giving none of my nerves away.

Need flashes in Dominique's eyes as he drinks me in. Then, without saying a word, he turns, jerks my bedroom door open, and leaves, slamming it shut behind him.

My phone rings but it takes me a minute to collect myself. I pick up Dominique's shirt from the floor and slip it on. Not because I want to wear anything that belongs to him, but because it's there. And then I dig my phone out of my bag. It's no longer ringing, but I can see it was my mom who called. I'll call her back later. I'm not really in the mood for one of her chats.

I consider going back to the party, but that doesn't sound appealing either, so instead, I drop down on my bed and crack open a textbook, telling myself that my decision to stay inside has nothing to do with Dominique. I just need to catch up on some homework.

Clearly, I am a big fat liar.

15

Dominique

There are only a few blocks between the Kappa Mu house and my place, so I walk, needing some time to clear my head. If I didn't get out of there when I did, I was going to do something I couldn't take back. I wouldn't regret it. I know that much. Taking Kasey and laying her down on her bed, sliding into her wet heat, yeah, that isn't something I would regret. But it is something that would make shit complicated, and I can't do complicated right now. Almost to my street, I change course and head for the field instead. I could use a run. My body is wound up tight. I need to tire myself out and get Kasey out of my head.

Three miles in and I still can't get the image of her naked body out of my mind. Sweat drips down my back, my calves burning, but I keep up the pace. Two more miles and my chest is heaving, but I still see her perfect tits. Her tiny waist. Her bare pussy. Running isn't going to cut it.

I jog off the track and head for my place. Maybe a cold shower will help.

When I reach my door, I notice Aaron's ride in the driveway, which means he's home. Good.

"Hey, man. You good?" I ask as soon as I see him.

He looks up, eyes bloodshot and unfocused.

I curse. "What happened?"

He shakes his head.

I grab a water bottle from the fridge, uncap it, and bring it back to him. He accepts it but doesn't take a drink. "Bro, you're freaking me out. What happened?"

His hands flex. "I freaked out, alright."

"I'm gonna need you to give me a little more information."

He hangs his head, no longer meeting my eyes. "A car pulled up to me while I was driving. They had music going. I—" He swallows hard. "There were gunshots in the song. I didn't think. Just fucking panicked."

Shit. "But you came home? You're good? Nothing else happened?"

He exhales a harsh breath. "Yeah. I'm good. Just freaked the fuck out."

"Why didn't you call? I would have come back sooner." I rub the back of my neck. He can't keep going like this. He needs help. Like real, professional help. "I think you should see someone—"

"I'm not talking to a fucking shrink."

I open my mouth to argue with him, but a phone buzzing halts my response. Aaron frowns down at his phone, the thing still buzzing.

"Who is it?" I ask.

He shakes his head. "No clue." He lifts the phone to his ear and answers. "Hello?"

"I'm gonna grab a quick shower," I tell him and head down the hall. I make it quick and cold. Enough time to wash the sweat from my body and erase the images of Kasey from my head so my dick calms the fuck down. That finished, I throw on a clean pair of clothes and head back to check on Aaron.

He still has the phone to his ear, but all the blood has drained from his face as he listens to whoever is talking.

"You okay, man?"

It's like he doesn't even hear me. His eyes fill with moisture and my chest seizes. *Fuck.* His hand falls away from his face, the phone still cradled in his palm. Whoever is on the other line is still speaking, but Aaron's no longer listening. I reach for the phone and he relinquishes it without comment.

I bring it to my ear right as he drops his head in his hands, a sob wracking his entire body.

"Who the hell is this?" I snarl.

There's a pause. "Are you related to Mr. Henderson," a calm voice asks almost hesitantly.

"I'm his roommate. What's going on? What did you say to him?" He's not in the right headspace to deal with whatever shit this is right now.

The guy on the other line clears their voice. "I'm sorry to be the bearer of bad news. I was explaining to Mr. Henderson—"

"Aaron," I correct.

"Right. I was explaining to Aaron that there's been an accident." I wait. "His... his mother was in a car accident on the highway earlier today. There was a pileup, and while Ms. Douglas was able to stop before colliding with the vehicle in front of her, the eighteen wheeler behind her wasn't able to do the same."

Fuck.

"Is she okay?"

He's quiet for a beat, and I look down at Aaron. He's hunched over, elbows on his knees and hands on the back of his head. If she was okay, he wouldn't be like that.

"She was rushed to Mercy Hospital but was DOA."

"What the hell does DOA mean?" I bite out, and it's Aaron who answers, his voice dejected.

"Dead on arrival."

"What?" I ask him, eyes wide before repeating into the phone, "What? She's dead?"

Aaron flinches.

"I'm sorry. She's gone. Aaron Henderson is listed as her next of kin. I was contacting him so we can proceed with the next—"

"No. He's not dealing with that today. He just found out his mom is gone. Everything else can wait."

"Sir, if I—"

"No. You can call back in a few days. Give the man some time to grieve." I hang up and toss Aaron's phone on the sofa beside him.

"Hey." He's not looking at me. "What do you need, man? What can I do?"

He hiccups and then gets to his feet.

"Whoa. Slow down. Where are you going?" He grabs his keys and heads for the door, but I block him. "Aaron—"

"I have to tell my sister. *Shit.* How am I supposed to tell her? How do—"

Fuck. I didn't even think about Kasey. Shit. "Okay. It's okay. You don't have to do that right now. We have time."

"Yeah, I do," he shouts, tears tracking down his face. I've never seen him like this before, and fuck if I know how to fix it. "She needs to know. She'd want to know. Now. Not tomorrow or in a few hours. She needs to know now. But how the fuck am I supposed to do that, Dom? She's my baby sister and I have to tell her but—"

I nod my head and grab him in a tight embrace. He clings to me like his life depends on it, hands fisted in the back of my shirt. "I get it, man. But, you're still processing shit right now. You can't drive like this. Just, sit down for a few, okay. We'll sort this out."

His shoulders shake. "She needs to know, man." His voice is hoarse.

"I'll tell her. You stay here and I'll tell her."

He pulls back and runs his hands through his hair, tugging on the strands as he begins to pace.

"You're cool with that? You don't mind?" he asks, not looking at me.

"I got you. I'll tell her. You stay here. I'll have the guys—"

"I don't need a babysitter," he grinds out.

"No, you don't. But you just lost your mom and you don't need to be alone right now either."

He shakes his head, about to argue.

"What about Allie?" I ask. They've always been close, and she lost her mom a few years back. She'll know how to help him get through this while I ... shit. I don't know how I'm going to break this to Kasey.

"Just, Allie?" he croaks.

"Yeah, man. Just Allie."

A nod.

"Okay. I'll call her. Just sit down. Okay?"

Another nod.

I pull out my phone and make the call. An hour later, there's a knock at our door and I let her inside.

"Hey, how's our boy doing?" she asks, voice low.

I peer over my shoulder at the boy in question. "He hasn't moved since I called you. Hasn't talked either."

She nods as I grab my keys. "Where are you going?"

I swallow past the lump in my throat. "He asked me to tell Kasey."

Her eyes soften and she places a hand on my arm. "Dom, that's ... you shouldn't have to—"

"I know. But he can't, and someone needs to."

"I can call Bibiana."

I shake my head. "No. I've got this. You look after him. Don't leave him alone or let him go anywhere by himself. If you need to call Roman to sit on him, do that, okay?"

She nods but..."I'm serious, Allie. He's dealing with some other shit right now too. His mom dying is awful, but the timing couldn't have been worse. Do not leave him alone. I'll handle Kasey, but depending on how she handles things, I don't know what time I'll be back. If you have to leave—"

"I got it. He won't be left alone."

"Good." I leave Allie with Aaron and jump in my Escalade. When I pull up to her place, it hits me that I don't know what I'm going to say to her, so I sit there, my car idling. It's been a few hours since I left and I know she won't be happy to see me but... it doesn't matter. I told Aaron I'd have his back and tell her, so I'm going to do that. He shouldn't be the one to drop this bomb on her. I've got this.

There's a back entrance off the hall that leads to Kasey's room, so I put my ride in drive and head that direction. There's a chance Kappu Mu's pool party is still in full swing. Greek parties are usually an all-day, all-night sort of thing. I don't want to see anyone and deal with their bullshit, so I'll slip into Kasey's room and wait for her there if she isn't inside already.

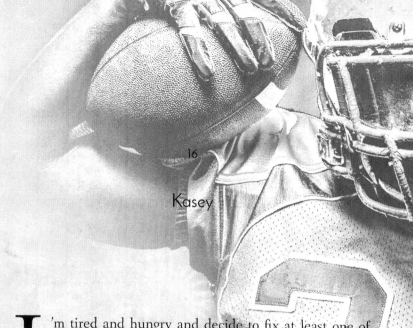

16

Kasey

I'm tired and hungry and decide to fix at least one of those problems by grabbing a bagel from the kitchen. I probably should have put pants on but I doubt anyone is going to come inside, and at least I bothered to slip underwear on before heading to the kitchen.

Dominique's shirt hangs down to the middle of my thighs, which is more than the swimsuit was covering. I should shred the damn thing. All I've had these past few hours is time. Time to think about how twisted up I am about a guy who clearly doesn't give a shit about me. I'm not this person, so why am I letting him get to me?

Decision made, I'm done letting him tell me what to do, or wear. I'm done giving a shit about his feelings or worrying about whether or not he's interested in me. I'm over it.

I'm going to focus on school. I'll date. Yes, I'll definitely date. Maybe Quinn or one of the other girls can fix me up with someone. I need to get over whatever it is that I feel for that asshole.

The toaster dings and I retrieve my bagel, dropping it on a plate before spreading a thin layer of butter on it. Next I add a layer of jelly. I know you're supposed to use cream cheese, but I'm not a huge fan and this tastes a whole lot better. The door leading to the backyard opens and Deacon steps inside.

"Hey," he says upon seeing me right as I bite into my bagel.

I give him a wave and point to my mouth as I chew. He nods and a few seconds later I swallow. "Sorry. Didn't want to talk with my mouth full."

"No problem." He shifts uncomfortably.

"So..." I say.

"Yeah. Sorry. I was just coming in to use the bathroom."

I point down the hall. "First door on your right."

He nods. "Thanks."

"No problem." He goes to take care of business and I put the butter and jelly back in the refrigerator. I take another bite of my bagel and grab a napkin before turning back to the fridge for a bottle of water. Hands full, I head back for my room right as Deacon exits the bathroom. "Have fun," I tell him as I slip past.

"Oh, hey, wait up."

I slow my steps, but I don't stop entirely. "What's up?"

"I was hoping we could talk," he says.

"I thought we already did?" We pause outside my room. I have a bagel in one hand and the water in the other so I'll need to shift things around to free up a hand, but I have a feeling if I open my door, he'll want to come inside, and I'm not sure that's a good idea. Deacon is nice, and hot. But I'm in a weird head space right now, and yes, I definitely want to get over whatever hang-up I have for Dominique at the moment, but I know myself. I'll do something reckless, like throw myself at the guy and just make a bigger mess out of things, which isn't fair to him. I need to find a guy not on the football team. One Dominique can't screw with to get at me.

"We did, it's just—" My door swings open on its own. Correction, the jerkface standing inside my room opens it.

"Leave," he says to Deacon, right as I say, "What the hell are you doing in my room?"

Dominique doesn't look at me, his penetrating stare resting solely on Deacon.

"Look, man..."

Dom shakes his head. "I don't have time to deal with you right now. You need to go. Now."

Deacon's shoulders are stiff as the guys stare off with one another. *Screw this.*

"Hi. I have a better idea. How about you both leave. That'd be great."

Deacon looks down at me, a flicker of hurt in his eyes, and I wince. "Sorry," I tell him. "This one brings the bitch out in me."

That seems to satisfy him, but still, neither guy moves. I turn to Dom. "Why are you even here?" I just decided I'm done with his crap and this is what the universe does? It'd be bad enough if he showed up on my doorstep, but in my room? Really?

Dom looks down at me. "We need to talk."

I scoff. "Pass. I don't have anything to say to you." The universe can shove it for all I care.

He gives me a once over, a smirk curling the corners of his mouth when he sees I'm wearing his shirt. "That looks good on you." He fingers one of the sleeves.

I smack his hand away with my bottle. "Go home, Dom."

"Kasey." There's a warning there.

"She said go home, man. Take the hint and back off."

Surprising me, Dom ignores him. Well, I guess that isn't really surprising, but I expected a verbal jab or maybe even a punch after that comment.

"I just want to talk—"

"No," I snap. Honestly, I don't want to talk to either of them. I want to eat my bagel and then I want to go to bed.

"No?" He rears back incredulously.

"You heard me. No. You were a complete asshole today. You were an asshole last week. You keep fucking with me and for what? I'm tired of this game, Dom. So, no, I don't want to talk to you. Not today. Not tomorrow. Just, go away."

He exhales a harsh breath and his eyes soften the slightest bit. "Kasey, I..." He pauses and turns to Deacon. "Look, I don't like you, but I need to talk to her about personal shit. So, you gotta bounce. Now."

Deacon's jaw tightens, but he nods. "Fine. But only if you get the team to stop fucking me over in practice."

"Done."

A nod. A handshake. And then Deacon leaves, and wasting no time, Dominique pulls me into the room and closes the door behind me.

"Just because you got rid of Deacon doesn't mean I'm going to talk to you. You can go, too," I tell him, setting my water and bagel down on the nightstand.

He sighs, and I know he's going to try again, but I've had time to think and I'm done. I want off his merry-go-round. "What part of go are you not understanding?"

His Adam's apple bobs. "It's about your mom."

A strangled laugh escapes me and I swing my arms wide. "What? What about her is so important that you had to come fuck up my night after already screwing my day?"

He doesn't say anything, just looks at me like I'm a little crazy and so what, maybe I am, but he made me this way. He's the one butting into my life. Interjecting himself where he doesn't belong, and now this.

"Well? What was so damn important that you couldn't just leave me the fuck alone?" He's not leaving. Fine. I'll leave instead. I grab a pair of leggings—I'll throw them on in the car —slip on some sandals, and grab my phone and keys. Jerking my bedroom door open, I head for the side door.

"Kasey!" He calls my name, but I don't stop.

"Go home, Dom," I call over my shoulder as I make it outside.

A few of the girls are outside hanging out on the picnic table. All of them looking my way as I exit the house, Dominique right behind me.

"Kasey, stop."

I flip him off over my shoulder and he growls. Actually growls. I'm almost to my car when he grabs me by the elbow, and I'm about to tear away from him when he bites out,"Your mom was in an accident."

"What?" I shake my head and pull away. "She literally called today while you were in my room earlier."

"Kasey," his voice is soft, eyes somber. A stab of pain hits me in the chest. No. He's wrong. I just talked to her a few days ago and she was fine. And she called earlier today. He doesn't know what he's talking about. I pull out my phone and punch in her number.

"Kasey—"

I hold my finger up, silently telling him to wait.

The call goes straight to voicemail. My stomach sinks, but no, that doesn't mean anything. Mom is forgetful. Her phone is probably dead. Once she charges it, she'll see the missed call and call me right back. It's fine. Everything is fine.

A notification flashes across the screen. I have a voicemail. I smack my forehead. Of course I do. She called earlier and left me a message. I enter my pin and wait for the message to start.

"Hey, sweetheart. I just wanted to check in on my girl. Hope you're having fun. I'll call yo—" her voice cuts off. There's the sound of tires squealing in the background. A shrill scream. The crunch of metal.

Oh my God! "Mom!" No. No. No. She has to be okay. She— Dominique reaches out, but I slap his hand away. I need to find my brother. I need... I drop my phone and shove past him. "Kasey, stop."

I don't. I move for my car, but strong arms band around me, turning me until we're face to face. "I'm sorry. I didn't know how else to tell you."

I shove against his chest, but he doesn't budge. Instead, he holds me tighter against his chest, one hand cupping the back of my head. "I'm sorry, baby girl. I'm so fucking sorry."

I shake my head. "No!" My vision blurs, but I blink back the tears. "*Never let them see you cry, sweetheart.*" Mom's words echo in my head.

I sniff and pull away. This time, he lets me go. "She's fine though, right? She's at a hospital or whatever? She's getting treatment?" I rub my eyes with the backs of my hands.

He doesn't say anything. He just stands there looking at me with eyes full of what ...regret?

"Well?" I shout. "You can talk now. That's why you're here, right? Is she going to be okay?" I need to talk to my teachers. If Mom is hurt she'll need someone to look after her. At least until she's back on her feet. I don't know how much time I can miss from school, but I'll figure that out later. Aaron will —*shit*. I need to talk to my brother. Does he know Mom was in an accident?

"Where's Aaron?"

"He's at home."

I frown. "Does he know Mom was hurt? I have to call him."

"He knows," Dominique says. "The hospital called him."

Okay. Good. She's at a hospital. That's good. But, "Why isn't he here? Why are you here telling me about my mom instead of him?" Anger floods my system and I latch onto it.

A tormented look flashes across his face. "He's having a hard time with the news. I don't..." he takes a deep breath, "He didn't know how to tell you."

"Is he packing at least?" I run through my mental to-do list. Pack some clothes. Notify my teachers that I have a family emergency. Book a flight to Florida. *Shit.* I don't even have the new address.

I'll figure that out once I talk to Aaron. I whirl around to go back inside. "Where are you going?"

"I need to pack."

"Kasey!"

"Dominique. I don't have time. If Mom is hurt, I need—"

"She didn't make it."

Something squeezes my chest and all the air whooshes out of my lungs. "W...what?"

My knees shake and everything suddenly sounds far away.

Dominique steps toward me, but it's almost like he's out of focus. My vision is dark along the edges.

"What do you mean, she didn't make it?" My voice is quiet, almost like if I say the words too loud it will make them real. But they can't be real. Mom is fine. She has to be fine.

"I'm so sorry," he tells me. This time, I believe him.

"No." I press the palm of my hand to my chest. "She can't ... no. She has to be okay. My mom," I choke back a sob. "No. She has to be okay!"

Dominique steps closer, his hands reaching out almost like I'm a wild animal he's afraid to spook.

"It's going to be okay."

"No, it's not. It is not going to be okay. This is not okay!"

"Fuck. I know. I'm sorry. That was the wrong thing to say."

I can't breathe. I'm opening and closing my mouth, trying to suck in air, but it's like my lungs have stopped working. I'm like a fish stuck on shore and I can't fucking breath.

"Kasey? Fuck. Kasey!"

A large hand forces my head between my knees. I didn't realize I'd fallen to the ground. "Breath, baby girl. In and out. That's good. Take another breath."

I try to focus on his words, but my chest hurts. It really really hurts.

He rubs circles across my back as I fight to get my emotions under control, but as soon as I manage to suck in a full breath, the tears come pouring out. A distant part of me is screaming to get it together. To push him away and find somewhere private to cry, but I can't move. I want to get up, but it's like the part of my brain that controls my limbs isn't working.

Strong arms scoop me up and the next thing I know I'm nestled in Dominique's arms as he walks me to his Escalade. My entire body shakes like a leaf. *She's gone. She's really gone.* The realization slams into me like a freight train and a new wave of tears falls down my cheeks.

Dominique sets me down on the passenger seat. How he opened the door while holding me, I don't know. He reaches over me and secures my seat belt before cupping my cheeks, his thumbs wiping the tears on my face. "You're going to get through this," he says, his voice somehow both soft and firm.

I hear the words, but I don't believe them. How does anyone get through something like this? How does anyone recover after losing their mom?

The rest of the night is a blur. Dominique takes me to his place, but I don't remember the drive there or even getting out of his Escalade and walking inside.

Aaron is there. Allie too. She hugs me, I think. I'm not really sure.

And then, nothing.

17

Kasey

"Kasey?"

I blink sleep from my eyes. Sunlight filters in through the window and it takes me a minute before I'm able to turn my head and find the person who said my name.

"Dom?"

He steps further into the room and I push up on my hands. I'm in bed. But, it's not mine. This bed is a queen but I know mine in my room at the Kappa Mu house is a full. "Whose bed is this?" I ask. My throat is dry and my words come out raspy.

Dominique sits down beside me, placing a hand on my leg. "You're in our guest room. You fell asleep, so I brought you here." He shrugs. "Figured this would be more comfortable than the couch."

That makes sense. "Thanks."

He stares at me intently before asking, "Are you feeling okay? Did you ... did you want to talk?"

I scowl. "Why would I want to—" Last night comes rushing back to me and I suck in a shuddering breath.

"Kasey?"

Oh God.

"Hey. Hey!" He cups both sides of my face and my vision swims. I'm crumbling, and he gets a front row seat to the show. "It's okay."

I shake my head. No. It's not okay. My mom is dead. I'm seventeen and she's fucking dead.

I pull away from his touch and turn to my side, resting my head on the pillow as silent sobs wrack my body. *Don't let him see you cry.* I tell myself. *You fucked that up yesterday. Don't make it worse. Hold it together.*

A rough hand rubs my back, but I pull away from the touch.

"Leave me alone," I whisper.

"Kasey." He sighs, and there's pity in his voice. It makes my tears fall faster. I don't want his pity. I just ... I want my mom.

Dominique leaves and I lose track of time after that. Day turns to night only to become day. It happens again and again, day after day. But, I barely move from the bed. I get up to use the bathroom. Sometimes I get up and sit by the window and look outside. The last time I did that I fell asleep, only to wake as Dominique laid me back in bed.

He brings me water. A few times he's tried to get me to eat but I'm never hungry. He's being nice to me and I hate it. This isn't how our relationship works. It's not helping me. It just makes it all worse.

The door to my room opens and I know without rolling over to look that it's Dominique who's come inside. I haven't seen Aaron since I got here. He's dealing with his own grief. Neither one of us is really equipped to help the other right now. I feel like a shitty sister about that, but I'm pretty sure he feels like a shitty brother too, so I figure we're square.

"How are you feeling?" He always asks the same question as if he doesn't already know the answer, so like all the other times, I don't bother to respond.

Dominique sighs and moves around the bed. He crouches down in front of me but I keep my eyes closed, hoping he'll take the hint and go away.

"You're not really asleep."

So? I want to tell him, but I stay quiet.

Another sigh. "The girls are here."

That catches my attention and I snap my eyes open. Dominique is eye level with me, his penetrating stare burning into me.

"They're worried about you. You're not responding to any of their texts."

"I don't want to talk to anyone," I whisper, my mouth so dry the words come out scratchy and raw.

He hands me an uncapped bottle of water. "Drink."

I shake my head. I don't want it.

"Kasey, drink the damn water or I'll hold you down and force it down your throat myself."

I glare at him, feeling mutinous. He waves the bottle in my face, his eyes daring me to push him.

"Fine." I pull myself up into a sitting position and take the bottle. Glaring at him, I swallow a few sips before giving it back. "Happy?" I ask and lay back down.

He grunts out a, "Yes," and places the water on the bedside table. "I told Allie and Bibi you were dealing, but you know how they can be. They want to see for themselves that you're okay. I think they mostly want to make sure I haven't buried you somewhere."

I suck in a breath.

"Fuck. Bad joke. Ignore that." He shakes his head. "I just thought you'd want a heads-up before they came in."

He moves to stand, but I latch onto his wrist, stopping him.

I swallow hard. "Don't let them in."

His eyes soften. "They're worried about you. We all are. It's been four days Kasey—"

I shake my head. "Please. I... I can't."

He looks away, a tic jumping along his jaw. "Allie lost her mom, too. She can help. Aaron's been spending a lot of time with her. Maybe—"

"No!"

He reaches down and tucks a strand of hair behind my ear, his fingers lingering on my cheek. "Okay. I'll tell them you need more time."

18

Dominique

"**S**he needs more time," I tell Allie, who gives me a worried look.

"It's been days," she says, like I don't already know that.

"I know but she... she asked for more time. I'm not going to push her if she isn't ready."

Allie gives Bibiana a pointed look. "Maybe we can—"

"B, no. She said no. The answer is no." Neither girl looks happy with my answer.

"She has classes. She's—"

"I spoke with the admin. They notified her teachers of the situation."

Allie's eyes widen. "Oh. Wow. That was really thoughtful of you."

I grunt. "She's got enough to worry about." They both do.

Aaron's in the other room, phone held up to his ear. He's been handling funeral arrangements. Trying to get the body transported back to Sun Valley so he can host a funeral, but it's a slow-going process with a lot of paperwork and hoops to jump through.

"How's he doing?" I ask Allie.

She purses her lips. "As good as can be expected. He's talking about it which is good. He's not holding everything in and letting the pressure build but—"

He snaps the phone shut and throws it across the room where it shatters against the wall. Yeah, he's handling shit well alright.

"Aaron?" I call, drawing his attention. "What's up?"

His chest is heaving as he fights to pull himself together. "I have to fly out to Florida. They won't release the body without me physically confirming it's her and signing off on some paperwork."

Fuck.

He runs his hands through his hair, his movements agitated.

"When do you need to go?" I ask.

"As soon as I can get there. I need to check flights and—"

"I got it."

He frowns.

"Peretti and Price has a company jet. I'll set it up. Just tell me when."

He swallows hard and nods. "Thanks, man."

"No worries. You want me to go with you?"

He looks at the door leading to the guest room, and I know what he's thinking. I don't like the idea of leaving Kasey alone any more than he does, but the thought of him dealing with this alone doesn't sit well, either.

"You should talk to her," I suggest, but he shakes his head. "I'm serious, man. She could use her big brother."

"How does that help her? I can't tell her it's going to be okay when I don't believe it myself, man. So what can I do? How can I fix this, because as far as I see it, I can't." He hangs his head and walks out of the room, his shoulders hunched and head hanging low.

"One of us can go with him," Allie says. "You take care of our girl. They'll get through this."

I want to believe her, but it's been four days since I brought Kasey back to our place. Four days and she's barely moved from the guest room. She's not eating. She never talks. It's like the girl has gone catatonic. I don't know what to do and Aaron's been fucking worthless, not that I can blame the guy.

He's either gone to Allie and Roman's or he's locked in his room, and now he's going to fly to Florida. How long will that take? How much longer can Kasey hide before shit gets serious?

"Yeah, okay. I'll make some calls and set up his flight. Just ..." I hesitate, but someone else needs to know. I can't watch them both twenty-four seven. "Can I talk to you for a sec?"

Without needing to be asked, Bibiana excuses herself. "I'm going to head home. Call me if she changes her mind and wants to talk, okay?"

I nod and give her a quick hug goodbye, being careful of her swollen belly. She has a few months left, but already she looks ready to pop. When she's gone, I turn to Allie and consider what to tell her.

"Aaron's been dealing with ... things."

She raises a brow. "Yeah. His mom just died."

I shake my head. "More than that. I can't tell you the how or why. I shouldn't be telling you any of this so don't repeat it, not even to Roman. Okay?"

She nods, worry crossing over her face.

"Aaron has PTSD."

She opens her mouth to ask a question, but I raise my hand to stop her. "Like I said. I can't tell you the why or the how. That's his story to tell when he's ready, but it's been getting worse. He wasn't handling it well before his mom died and now, well, it's not going to get any better. He's just ignoring one problem in place of the other, and eventually the other shoe is going to drop. He doesn't sleep enough. He gets these night terrors where he wakes up panicked and drenched in sweat. And loud noises can set him off. Almost like a panic attack where he feels like the walls are closing in."

"Has he talked to anyone?"

I shake my head. "He won't see a shrink. I've tried but he refuses. I just... you need to know what to look out for because he's getting worse, not better."

She nods. "Okay. What do I need to know."

Fuck. Where did I even begin? "He needs to be in a relaxed environment as much as possible. No parties. No loud, sudden noises. He tries to push it. He thinks if he exposes himself to the shit that sets him off that it'll desensitize him to it, but that doesn't work. Video games with shooters can be a trigger. The smell of smoke. If he doesn't sleep for more than three days he's got pills he's supposed to take to help with that. They knock him out, but he wakes up feeling hungover so he doesn't like taking them, but if he's not sleeping he has to. It gets worse when he doesn't."

She nods. "Okay. I can look out for that."

I take a breath and tell her the last thing. "If you startle him, he can lash out. Physically. He pulls himself back once he recognizes you but he's landed a punch a time or two. For me, that's not a problem. With you or another chick, it will be. Don't surprise him. If you walk in a room and he's spacing out, call his name. Don't touch him until he acknowledges you. Got it?"

"Yeah. I got it."

"Good. I'm gonna make a few calls and get that flight sorted out. Let me know if shit changes with him or if you need me for anything else."

She nods and I go to my room to make the call. My parents will kill me for this. Not because they give a shit if I use the jet, but because we had an agreement I wouldn't use Price assets unless I was willing to be an active member of the family—which I'm not—but it'll take them a while to notice, and what they don't know won't hurt them. It'll just bite me in the ass later.

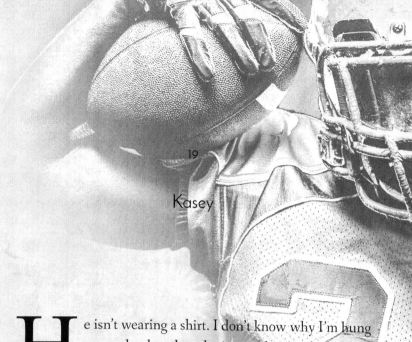

He isn't wearing a shirt. I don't know why I'm hung up on that but there he is, standing in the kitchen barefoot, wearing gray sweatpants without a shirt on.

I somehow manage to step farther into the room. He's at the stove, spatula in hand and he's making ... I peer around him ... pancakes. Dominique is making pancakes. What twilight zone did I just walk out of?

"You're up," he says without turning around.

I clear my throat. "Yeah."

"Have a seat. I'm almost done."

I nod, not that he sees it, and take a seat at the kitchen island, watching the muscles in his back flex as he moves around the kitchen, grabbing syrup and peanut butter before plating the pancakes and setting everything down in front of me.

"You hungry?"

I shake my head.

"When's the last time you ate?"

I think about it, but I don't really remember. "How long has it been since ..." I can't say it, but he knows what I mean and curses.

"You need to eat. I brought food to your room. Why didn't you eat any of it?"

"I'm not hungry."

"I don't care." He tosses two pancakes onto a new plate, spreads peanut butter on both and then drizzles them with syrup before sliding it across the counter to me. "Eat."

I stare down at the food. My stomach twists into a knot and my eyes fill with moisture.

"Dammit." He walks around the counter until he's right beside me. "You're wasting away. You need to eat something. Just a few bites, okay?"

I nod, forcing back the tears. I pick up the fork and knife and cut into the pancakes.

Dominique grabs his own plate and fills it with bacon, eggs, and a single piece of toast. But no pancakes. I frown down at my plate. "Why aren't you having any pancakes?"

"Not on my meal plan."

"Then why did you make pancakes if you knew you weren't going to eat any?"

He grunts. "You order pancakes every time we go to Sun Valley Station. Figured if I was going to get you to eat something, this was my best bet. You mentioned before that pancakes were your favorite food group."

"You remembered that?"

He nods.

I smile at that. Pancakes are my favorite food group. Mom used to make them on Sundays. Always with peanut butter and syrup, how her mom used to make them when she was growing up.

A fresh wave of grief sweeps over me and I blink back the tears, eyes locked on my plate.

Dominique either doesn't notice or chooses not to mention it, which I'm grateful for. "I have practice today. I missed earlier this week, which was fine. Coach wanted me to take it easy because of my shoulder anyway, but we have a game tomorrow and I have to show up. Will you—"

"I'll be fine."

He frowns. "That's not what I was going to ask."

Oh. "What were you going to ask?"

He looks at me, looks at my plate, then waits. I sigh and take a bite.

He grunts. "I was going to ask if you'd come to campus with me. Aaron had to fly out to Florida to take care of a few things and I don't like the idea of leaving you here alone."

"I—"

He cuts me off. "There's a lounge area just off the locker rooms where you can hang out. Maybe catch up on homework or watch some brainless T.V. on the television inside. We usually watch game tapes but I think Coach has it hooked up to cable."

I worry my lower lip. "I'd rather stay here."

His muscles flex and he takes a bite of his food, chewing while he thinks. "Practice is less than two hours. I can leave early if I need to. You won't have to be there long."

I shake my head. "I don't want to go. I never should have gotten up. I'll just go back to the room and—"

"Kasey, I'm not leaving you here alone. Right now isn't the time for you to be difficult. Change your clothes if you want."

I look down at myself. I'm still wearing his shirt. It's been several days. Almost a week and I'm still in the same shirt. The same pair of underwear. Oh god. I probably smell.

"If it's quick, you have time for a shower."

I swallow hard and nod. "Fine."

"Really?"

"Yeah. But I want a shower first."

He exhales a harsh breath. "Okay. Good. Eat some more first. We'll leave in an hour."

I take another bite, barely tasting it, but it seems to make him happy. My stomach growls, so I must be hungry. I just don't *feel* hungry. I'm numb. Empty.

I force myself to eat one whole pancake before pushing my plate aside. "I need to go back to my place. I don't have any clothes or—"

"Your uh, big sister, what's her name?"

"Quinn."

"Right. She packed up some of your things. Clothes. Toiletries. They're in the bag on the bathroom counter. If you're missing anything we can stop by and grab it on the way."

Oh. That was nice. "Okay. I'll go see what I've got." I hesitate. "After practice, are you taking me home?"

Some emotion flashes in his eyes, too fast for me to catch before he shakes his head. "No. You're going to stay here." Something like relief settles in me, but that's strange. Why would I be relieved about staying here? I don't like Dominique. We were literally fighting just a few days ago.

"For how long?"

He shrugs and goes back to his plate. "Until I decide you're okay."

My mouth tightens, and I consider arguing before my shoulders sag and I turn away. "Fine." I head for the bathroom to shower. I'll fight with him another day.

Dominique parks the Escalade near the athletic building, and before I even unbuckle, he has my door open and is helping me out of the car.

Why is he being so nice? Nice and Dominique Price don't go together. I mean, I know my mom just... the word stalls in my brain and I take a moment to breathe through it. Whatever the reason, I don't want him to be nice to me. I need things to be normal. I don't want his or anyone else's pity.

I tug my hand out of his as soon as I'm out of the car. He grabs a gym bag from the back and then we're cutting across the parking lot to the main doors. Inside, I ignore the students in the halls and follow Dominique to the locker room. He opens the door and loud voices can be heard. Blocking my sight, he takes me down a row of lockers before stopping at a closed door. He pushes it open and checks inside before backing up and holding it open for me.

"Yo, Price!" someone calls.

"Give me a minute," he shouts back. To me he says, "You can hang out here. No one will bother you."

We step into a medium-sized room. There are a few sofas scattered around the room and a large flat screen T.V.

mounted on one of the walls. "There's a bathroom through that door." He points to the left. "And I'll have Coach hang on to my phone. If you need anything, call me. I'll be done in an hour and a half. Two, tops."

I nod and take a seat on the nearest sofa.

"You're not going to wander off, right?"

"I'll be here."

He stares at me as if gauging my intent. "Good. If any of the guys come in here, tell them to get the fuck out. Got it?"

"Yep."

He closes the door behind him and I take a steadying breath. I find a remote between the cushions and flick on the T.V., stopping on a Disney movie. I don't have it in me to watch anything heavier than that. My phone rings. Aaron's name flashes across the screen. Shit. I haven't even talked to my brother yet. I should have. But I haven't.

I'm not sure what to say to him, and I'm almost certain he hasn't known what to say to me, but he's in Florida handling things I know I'm not in the right headspace to handle, so I need to answer.

I hit accept and bring the phone to my ear. "Hey."

He's quiet on the other end before I hear him release a breath. "Hey."

That one word, hearing his voice, has emotions clogging my throat. "You good?" I ask.

He forces a laugh. "I should be asking you that."

Yeah. Maybe. "I'm okay."

Another heavy breath. "That's good. Dom's not being an asshole is he?"

A small laugh. "No. He's being nice, which is ... weird. I kinda wish he'd be an asshole."

I curl my legs beneath me and sink into the sofa. "Are you calling because..." I swallow hard. "Did you need..." I don't know how to get the words out.

"Yeah. Sorry. I wanted to ask if you were okay with Mom being cremated. It's a lot easier to get her back if we do but if you don't want that—"

"It's fine," I choke on the words.

"Are you sure?"

"MmHmm." My heart squeezes in my chest. We weren't very religious, but I know Mom is—was—Catholic. She'd have wanted a proper burial, but I don't think either Aaron or I can go through with one. This, this is better. "Maybe we can sprinkle her ashes in the ocean or something. Mom might have liked that."

"You think so?" His voice is thick.

I have to blink back my tears before I can answer. "Yeah. I think she would. Remember when we were kids and we went to Myrtle Bay? You got stung by a jellyfish and freaked out trying to pee on your own leg."

He groans, but manages a laugh too. "You promised never to bring it up again."

I snicker. "I know, but we should go there. We used to go every summer growing up. Mom loved that place."

"Yeah, she did, didn't she?"

I sit still, holding the phone tight as we both listen to the other breathe. "I miss her," I tell him, hating how my voice quivers.

"I miss her, too."

This is hard. My eyes fill with tears again, and no matter how hard I fight to hold them in, they still spill down my face. "Will you be home soon?" I ask, needing to say something to fill the silence.

He coughs, clears his throat. "Yeah. I'll be back in a few days. We can figure out what to do after that. There's no rush, okay. We can take however long we want."

I bob my head up and down. "Okay."

"I gotta go, but I'll try and check in later. You'll be okay with Dominique?"

I swallow past a lump. "Yeah. I'll be okay."

"I love you, sis."

"Love you, too." Aaron hangs up and I just sit there, unmoving. I don't know for how long or what time it is when all of a sudden the door opens and Deacon steps in the room.

I look up at him, tears still running down my face and he drops down in front of me. "Hey, are you okay? Are you hurt?" He checks me over as I sit there, frozen in place.

"Kasey." He cups the sides of my face. "What's wrong? Why are you crying."

I look down at my phone. It's still in my hand, fingers gripping it tightly. Deacon sees it and gently pries it from my fingers, setting it beside me. "You're kinda freaking me out here," he says. "I saw you come in with Dominique, figured I'd check in on you. I can't believe he left you in here like this."

I shake my head. "He didn't. I—" *Come on Kasey, pull it together.* "I'm sorry." I blink. "I was just talking to my brother. I..."

His gold-colored eyes stare into me, seeing more than he should. I want to curl into a ball and hide. Turn off the lights and just pretend today isn't here. "Come on." He pulls me to my feet.

"Where are we going?"

"You need chocolate. Or cake. Or both. We're going to get some of that."

I side-eye him as he steers me out of the room. "Why do I need chocolate? And don't you have practice?"

He shrugs, his hand on my lower back as he leads me outside. "I have sisters. When they cry, I give them chocolate. It's the one thing I never get wrong and it works every time, so that's what we're going to do. Come one, there's a vending machine just down the hallway."

I nod but... "What about practice?"

"Dominique is running plays today, so it's fine. No one will miss me."

"Oh. Alright then." We find the vending machine and he shoves a few dollar bills in getting a Reese's, Snickers, Hershey bar, Milky Way, and a Fast Break. Arms full, we find a few lounge chairs to sit in and he drops the candy in my lap.

When I don't move to open any, he grabs one of the bars, a Snickers, and peels the wrapper back before handing it to me. "Try it. I swear it works."

I give him a disbelieving look, but take a bite anyway, letting the chocolate melt on my tongue. I chew and swallow before taking another bite, and the next thing I know, the Snickers is gone and I'm moving onto the Peanut Butter Cups.

Three candy bars in and I feel more like myself. I've wiped the tears from my face, and Deacon catches me up on some of what I've missed in our English class. Twenty minutes goes by, and for the first time in nearly a week I feel like I can breathe. This distraction, it's exactly what I need.

I look down at the last candy bar in my lap and know I'll regret it later, but I peel back the wrapper and take a bite anyway. I moan. Fast Breaks are my favorite, so I saved the best for last.

"You cannot make sounds like that," Deacon says, a small smile on his face.

I roll my eyes. "You'd moan if you had this in your mouth."

He chokes, but covers it with a cough. "You can't say things like that to me either."

I grin. "Want a bite?" I ask him, but a commotion down the hallway catches my attention and I turn. "Shit," I whisper. Dominique is storming toward us, shirt drenched in sweat and a pissed-off expression on his face.

He's already yelling before he's even next to me. "What the hell were you thinking?" he shouts, coming to a stop beside us. "Do you have any idea how worried I was when I opened the door and you weren't there? *Fuck.*" He turns around, hands on his waist and takes a few steps away before turning back to me. "You said you'd stay put. Why did you—" It's then that he notices Deacon. His eyes darken and I jump to my feet.

"Look, I'm sorry. I should have left a note or something."

He scoffs. "Right. A note would have helped."

My anger spikes. I'm not a child. I don't need to be coddled and looked after. "You know what, fine. I'm not sorry." I turn to Deacon. "Thanks for the chocolate and for helping with," I wave to my face, "all of this. It was nice to feel like me for a little bit."

He stands. "Anytime you need a good laugh and some chocolate, give me a call. You don't have to tell me your personal shit, but if you wanna hang, I'm around."

"Thanks. I appreciate that."

He pulls me in for a hug, releasing me just as quickly when Dominique makes a sound in the back of his throat, low and threatening. "I'll catch you later, beautiful," Deacon calls over his shoulder, and then it's just Dom and I.

I sigh and pick up the candy wrappers that fell when I stood up. I shove them in the trash bin and wait for Dominique to yell at me some more, but he doesn't. Instead, he has this pensive look on his face and he refuses to look at me. Somehow, it's worse than the yelling.

When we get outside he opens the door for me, closing it once I'm safe inside the Escalade. I put on my seat belt as he gets inside and I fiddle with the music knob as he pulls out of the parking lot. Five minutes into the drive and he still hasn't said anything.

I hate it.

"Look, I'm sorry. Okay? Can you stop giving me the silent treatment already?"

"I'm not giving you the silent treatment."

I huff. "Then why are you so silent?"

He glares at me. "Do you all of a sudden want to talk? You've barely said a word in five fucking days, but I leave you alone for an hour and suddenly you're chatting with Deacon. My bad. Figured I must be the one guy you refuse to talk to."

I lean my head against the window, the cool glass chilling my skin. "I'm not refusing to talk to you," I tell him.

He grunts. "But you'd rather talk to Deacon?"

"No. I..." I try to put my thoughts into words, but it all sounds so stupid. "Deacon isn't treating me differently."

Dominique scowls. "What the hell does that mean?"

"You're being nice. Like really nice. You check on me all the time. You made me pancakes. You open my door for me."

"So what, I'm supposed to be a dick even though your mom just died?"

My breath hitches and Dominique mutters a curse. "I didn't mean—"

"That," I yell at him. "That, right there. You keep doing things like that. You're apologizing to me when before, you never would have said 'I'm sorry.' That isn't you. That's not us. Not how we communicate."

"You're not making any sense."

"I don't want you to treat me any different. I need things to go back to how they were. The bickering. You being an insensitive jerk."

"I'm not insensitive."

"Yeah, you are. You kissed me when we were in high school and pretended like it never happened. You told me I was shallow. That I couldn't keep a guy's attention. And then gave me the best orgasm of my life, and after, pretended like it never happened. You humiliated me at the Kappa Mu party, made me get out of the pool, basically said I looked like a slut and when I stripped naked in front of you, you left, and big surprise, you pretend it never happened. I'm sorry, how is none of that insensitive? Did you actually consider my feelings even once before doing any of those things?"

He's quiet.

"No. You didn't. And it's fine."

He bangs his head back on the headrest. "It's not fine."

"Yes, it is. It's fine because it's you. It's what I expect. You're a jerk to me. I'm a bitch to you. But this, whatever this version of you is that's nice to me, I can't deal with it right now. I need you to be the same guy you were a week ago. Don't coddle me. I'm not a piece of glass. I won't break."

We pull into his driveway and he turns off the car, neither of us getting out. "You want me to be a jerk."

"Yes."

"Fine. Your mom died almost a week ago, and you're being a baby. You've been hiding in your room for too fucking long and you're wasting away. You've lost weight. You look like shit. And your brother has enough on his plate that he has to deal with, but instead of handling what he needs to, he's calling me five times a day to check on you when he shouldn't have to. Pull yourself together, figure out what you need to do to grieve, and get on with it."

I suck in a shuddering breath and squeeze my hands into fists on my lap.

"Shit. I went too far."

I press my lips together, blinking back the tears and shaking my head. "I'm fine." I tell him, but it's a lie. There's this hole inside of me and his words, hearing about Aaron, it punches the hole wide open. I'm so fucking selfish. My brother shouldn't have to check in on me.

I fight to keep it together. I told Dom to be mean. He did what I asked, so why does it hurt?

He opens his door and the next thing I know he's right beside me, reaching over my lap to unbuckle me. "I'm sorry. I didn't mean any of it. I thought ... I thought this is what you wanted. I thought it would help."

Like a dam breaking, my tears fall down my cheeks.

"Fuck."

I was falling apart. Again. I had an hour where I kept it together and now I was crumbling.

Dom slides his arms beneath me and carries me out of the car. Cradled in his arms, he manages to get us inside and into the living room. My arms are wrapped around his neck, as though holding onto him will somehow hold me together.

He sits on the sofa, still cradling me in his arms. It's intimate and comforting and even knowing I'll hate myself for it tomorrow, I cling to him and cry into his chest.

I feel like pieces of me are breaking one by one, the pain growing more and more with each breath until it's too much. I want to scream, but nothing can get out past the tears. My shoulders shake and I wheeze, unable to catch my breath. Why does it hurt so fucking much.

"Kasey, please." He presses his lips to my temple. "You're killing me here, baby girl. What can I do?"

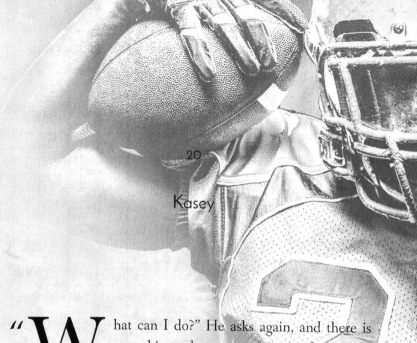

20

Kasey

"**W**hat can I do?" He asks again, and there is something close to panic in his voice. Emotion clogs my throat, threatening to suffocate me, and no matter how hard I try, I can't swallow it down.

I try to speak. To tell him it hurts too much. I don't want to live like this. But I choke on my words, unable to get them out. I scream, choking on my tears as Dominique holds me in place, a wild look in his eyes. One hand grips the back of my neck, the other clutches my hip. "Kasey, I don't know how to fix this. How to fix you. What can I do?" He is almost begging and Dominique never begs but ...

Nothing. There isn't anything he can give me that will make this go away. Nothing that will bring my mom back.

"I don't want to ... feel like... this. It hurts... too much," I finally manage to tell him.

He curses and a nerve jumps in his neck. "One night. I'll go to the store, get a fifth and you can drink yourself into oblivion if you need to, but only for one night. You got me? You get one pass. Will that help?" I nod. Yes. A night of oblivion. A chance to forget.

"Okay, we can do that but, for that to happen, I need to run to the store and I'm not leaving you here, alone like this. You have to come with me. You can wait in the car and I'll be quick, but I'm not leaving you here alone. Will that help? Do you want to forget for one night?"

I do. I really, really do, but it's a temporary fix. I know Dominique well enough to know he's serious when he says one night. That's all I'll get and tomorrow, when the sun rises, all my pain will still be there, only magnified by a hangover.

I pound my fists against his chest. "That's not—" a shuddering breath, "—enough."

"*Fuck.* Kasey, you have to work with me here."

I shake my head. No. "A week," I plead. "Let me forget for a week."

He moves his hands to either side of my face, leaning in until we're only an inch apart, our foreheads almost touching.

"No. You can't go down that path or you might not come back."

"I don't care," I wail.

"I do."

Tears spill from my eyes and hopelessness slams into me. "I hate you," I tell him. "I hate you. I hate you. I hate you."

"I hate you, too," he tells me, but the way he says it doesn't sound like he's telling me he hates me at all. It sounds like he's saying something else entirely.

"I don't want to feel like this anymore." I don't want to feel at all.

"I know, baby. I know. If I could make the pain go away, I would. Fuck, I'd do anything to make it go away right now."

There's that endearment again. I know it means nothing. He's just being nice to me. Using comforting words, but what if it's more than that? Or what if it can be more than that? At least for a little while.

I reach for him, shifting in his lap. "Please."

He holds me tight against his chest. "Anything, Kasey. Help me out here. What will make it bearable right now? This very moment? What else can I do? I can't see you like this and not do something. I have to do something."

I don't let myself think about it. I lean back in his embrace and when he tilts his chin down to look at me, his eyes full of concern, I kiss him.

He responds immediately, his hold shifting until he's grasping the side of my neck and angling me for a deeper kiss. Hot. Desperate. I pour everything I'm feeling into that kiss. My hurt. The pain. The anger over it all.

Our teeth clash. Our tongues duel. He slides his fingers into my hair and devours my mouth. There is no other way to describe it, and the longer he kisses me, the further the pain fades into the background. It's still there, lurking in the shadows of my mind. I'm not naive enough to think kissing Dominique will make it go away forever, but it helps. It gives me something else to think about. Something else to feel.

But, I need more.

I shift until I'm straddling his lap and rock myself against him.

He groans, breaking the kiss. "Kasey..."

I see my own need reflected back in his eyes. He wants this just as much as I do. We may not get along. Hell, we might even hate each other, but this, this he can do. This will help.

"Are you sure?"

My eyes narrow and I shift on his lap, grinding against the hard-on he's sporting beneath me. That should be his answer.

"Fuck."

He captures my mouth again. After that, it's a flurry of frenzied movements as we tear at one another's clothes.

He lifts my shirt off and cups my breast through the thin lace of my bra. I arch closer to his touch, throwing my head back as he squeezes me in his hand.

"We should move," he mumbles against my lips, but I don't let that deter me. I slide my hand into his sweats, wrapping my fingers around him and giving him a firm stroke.

"Jesus Christ," he hisses.

The next thing I know he's on his feet, my legs wrapped around him. He carries me to his room, closes the door behind him, and then tosses me on his bed, my back sinking into the soft mattress. He doesn't miss a beat. In a flash, he's on me. His powerful body pressing firmly against mine.

He kisses me again and I gasp, his tongue seeking out my own and sliding into my mouth. I moan. He tastes so good. Like coffee and spice. His shirt rubs against my skin and I immediately hate it. I don't want anything between us. I need to feel his skin on mine.

I claw at his shirt until he relents and tugs it over his head. Then I reach for the waistband of his sweats.

He smacks my hand away and seizes control. Unhooking my bra, he bares me to him before hooking his fingers into my panties and peeling them off. He doesn't bother with my skirt. What would be the point? With my breasts on full display, he runs his thumb over my nipple before sliding down my body to take one in his mouth.

I whimper.

He peppers kisses across my chest before swirling my other nipple with his tongue.

"Dominique, please."

He glances up at me, his eyes an even darker shade of brown than usual. He watches my face as he kneads my breasts, cataloging every gasp and moan I make. He pinches and pulls on my nipples.

"You're so fucking responsive."

My breathing is heavy as he slips further down the bed until his broad shoulders are nestled between my thighs. He spreads my legs open, and as his face stares down at my sex, his warm breath fans across my skin. I could die and go to heaven with the way he is looking at me right now, his gaze hot and hungry.

He doesn't give me the chance to speak. To get nervous. He locks his hooded gaze with mine and presses a hungry kiss to my core, using his thumbs to spread me open even more.

"Shit," I gasp.

He chuckles, sliding his hands under my thighs and cupping my ass as he tilts my pelvis closer to his mouth. "You like that?"

My teeth sink into my bottom lip, and I nod.

He leans in again and his mouth latches onto my pussy. I cry out, throwing my head back against the bed. He licks my slit before spearing his tongue inside me, and after only a few strokes, the pressure begins to build.

My pussy clenches and my legs quiver as he teases me, licking and sucking, but never putting enough pressure on my clit to throw me over the edge. I thrust my hips up to meet his touch, my body desperate for more friction.

I'm wound so tight I feel like I'm about to snap. "Dominique!"

He grabs my hips and begins to eat my pussy like a man starved. It only takes another minute until I'm crying out and bucking against him, but he doesn't let up. He locks onto my clit, my body hyper aware and overly sensitive as wave after wave of pleasure slams into me.

Limp and sated, my legs shamelessly drop to the bed. I struggle to catch my breath.

I expect Dominique to stop. To climb back beside me, but he stays rooted between my legs. His mouth still between my thighs. When I feel like my heart is no longer at risk of beating out of my chest, he flicks his tongue over my sensitive clit. I moan. Dominique presses his palm over my stomach, holding me down as he devours me all over again, only this time he nudges one thick finger inside me.

My muscles tense, legs quivering. I groan as he strokes me. "Oh, god."

"Fuck, you're tight," he murmurs against me right as a second orgasm hits me out of nowhere and I grind against his hand, riding out my release.

Dominique leans back, his eyes taking me in. "Better?" he asks, rising to his feet.

He still had his pants on. Why is he still wearing clothes?

Despite the fatigue, I push myself up to my elbows. My hair sticks to my neck and forehead and I brush it back away from my face. "Off," I tell him, and tilt my chin toward his pants.

He doesn't move. "Dominique," I growl. "Are you going to stand there or are you going to fuck me?"

His eyes darken, a savage expression passing over his face. "I don't think we—" He hesitates. "We don't need to do that. I can make you feel good in other ways."

Common sense dictates I listen. I haven't slept with anyone before, and a grief-induced fuck fest isn't how I imagined my first time, but I'm past the point of caring. I want this. Need it.

"If you don't want me—"

"I'm not saying that."

I swallow and can feel myself being pulled under again. A mess of emotions swirling inside me. No. No. NO!

I blink quickly as I bite out my words. "Then what are you saying?"

He rubs his jaw, my release still glistening on his lips. "You want me to fuck you?"

"Yes." I thought I made myself clear already. "I'm not going to force myself on you. If you don't want this, want me in this way, I can find someone else—"

"The hell you will," he snarls.

Dominique shoves his pants down and steps out of them, his cock hard and at attention. *Oh my god,* he's huge. A thread of doubt worms its way inside of me. Will it fit?

Without breaking eye contact, he leans to the side and retrieves a condom from the nightstand. He tears the foil packet with his teeth and shamelessly rolls the condom onto his shaft, before stroking himself.

"Say it again," he grinds out as he climbs onto the bed, positioning his cock at my slick entrance. "Tell me what you need."

"I need you to fuck me."

He makes an animalistic sound in his chest, and the head of his cock slides between my folds but without entering me.

"If you regret this in the morning—"

"I won't," I assure him.

Blind desire flashes across his face, but rather than sinking into me as I expect, he sits back on his heels and flips me onto my stomach. My heartbeat kicks into overdrive as he pulls my hips toward him until I'm on hands and knees.

"Dom," my voice quivers with need.

His cock rubs against me from behind.

I shift my hips back and turn my head to look at him. His face is locked in concentration, his expression almost predatory. "Spread your legs for me."

I do what he asks, widening my stance. He presses a hand against the center of my back. "Tilt your ass up," he orders, before sliding that same hand down between my legs. I try to tamp down on my nerves as Dominique presses a finger inside me, rubbing the walls of my pussy before he retreats and lines up his cock. Goosebumps break out across my skin and he leans forward, scraping his teeth over my bare shoulder as his hips thrust against me, his cock buried to the hilt in a single powerful move.

I cry out, a sharp stab of pain spearing into me.

He stills. "What the fuck?"

My legs tremble, but I manage to blindly reach back and grab hold of his wrist. "Don't."

"You're a virgin." He sounds both pissed off and in awe.

Not anymore. I think to myself, but don't say the words aloud.

"Why would you... why didn't... *fuck.*"

My body is tight, my muscles clenching against the intrusion. I force myself to take a deep breath and relax.

Dominique leans over me, his forehead resting between my shoulder blades. "What were you thinking?" he whispers against my skin.

"Dominique?" I say through clenched teeth.

"Yeah?"

"Move." He pulls back and for a second I think he's going to withdraw all the way. "Not stop," I clarify, and he stills. The head of his cock barely inside of me. "I need you to move."

He flexes his hips, an inch sinking back into me.

I moan.

He curses.

"Your first time shouldn't be like this," he growls. "It should be with someone you trust. Someone—"

"Dominique." I give him a second. Looking back, I meet his conflicted gaze. "I trust you."

His nostrils flare. "You do?"

I nod. "Yes. Now please, fuck me already." He sinks in another inch, his eyes carefully watching me for my reaction. He's stretching me to my limits and I can scarcely breathe.

He goes a little deeper.

My body is tight, my muscles clenching against the intrusion.

He pushes into me agonizingly slowly until he's sheathed himself fully. He gives my body a second to adjust and then he moves. In and out as he continues to thrust inside me. I grind my teeth together against the pain. It's not a lot, but enough to be uncomfortable. His body blankets me, his chin resting against my shoulder, breath against my ear. "Relax into it. Let me make you feel good."

I do what he says and force myself to relax, the tension in my body melting away to be replaced with tingling sensations. "That's it."

He leans back, hands gripping my hips as he increases his pace.

I gasp when he hits a particularly sensitive spot. I moan. My mind goes blank and all I can think about, all I can feel, is Dominique moving inside of me.

I push back on my knees, meeting him thrust for thrust, and then I'm coming again, my release spilling out of me on a guttural moan.

He slides out of me and flips me onto my back before sliding right back in, barely missing a beat. He hooks one arm under my knee, lifting my leg up and out to achieve a deeper angle.

I cling to his shoulders as he pounds into me, neither of us saying anything over the sounds of our flesh coming together. One of his hands cups the back of my neck and I stare into his eyes, even as I raise my hips to meet him.

His thrusts come faster, his face tight with tension as he surges inside me. "This what you need?" He forces out the words. I know what he's asking, so I don't hesitate to answer.

"Yes. More. Over and Over." I want to fall asleep from exhaustion. I don't want to lie here and think about my dead mom. About the pain or how helpless I feel. "Fuck me and don't stop. Okay? Not until I pass out. Until neither of us can go anymore."

A tremor moves through him and he nods. Good. We're in agreement.

His mouth crashes down on mine. His tongue licking against my own and his teeth scraping over my bottom lip. At some point the sun sets and the light coming through the windows dims. His forehead rests against my shoulder and my hands cling to his back, nails digging in when he stiffens and groans, pumping out his release.

He slumps against me, our breathing loud in the room. He takes a moment to catch his breath before sliding out of me. I hiss, but don't say anything. Dominique pulls off the condom, leaving to get rid of it before pulling another one out and setting it on the nightstand. I'm not sure how long a guy needs to recover, but he doesn't let me think on it long before he's reaching for me, his fingers sliding between my legs. First, he inserts one finger. Then a second. He works his fingers inside of me, rotating and rubbing every inch inside of me as he thrusts them in and out.

He adds a thirds and I cry out, his mouth crashing over mine and swallowing my cries.

I don't know how long he finger fucks me. Long enough for me to come again and for him to get hard. When he pulls out of me, he licks my juices from his fingers and slides the new condom over his cock.

He positions himself at my entrance again and I nod, letting him know I want this. Want more. He slides into me, a curse slipping past his lips.

"Yes," I tell him. "Don't stop."

We fuck two more times before we're both incapable of moving. After he disposes of the condom, I push up to leave. My legs feel like rubber and my head spins, but I think I can make it back to the guest room, only Dominique stops me.

He slips back into bed beside me and grabs me from behind, pulling my hips against his. My back to his front.

"Sleep," he grunts, tucking my head beneath his chin.

"But—"

"Sleep."

I take a deep breath, close my eyes, and for the first time in a long time, I do what Dominique tells me to do. I sleep.

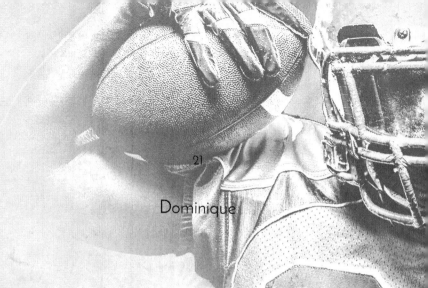

21

Dominique

I'm fucked. I am seriously and thoroughly fucked.

Harsh sunlight bleeds into the room. The clock on the wall reads eight AM. Late for me to be waking up, but not late enough that I need to hurry. Kasey is curled up in bed beside me, eyes closed, and blond hair fanning around her pillow. I close my eyes for a beat, breathing in the smell of her apple and vanilla shampoo. I stifle a groan. She smells *good*.

I take in her delicate shoulders, the way she fits perfectly nestled in my arms, her ass pressing against my front. My dick stirs to life.

The thought of rolling her over and sliding my cock inside her wet heat has my dick jumping to attention. I press my hips against her and she lets out a breathy little sigh, pressing deeper into me in her sleep. She feels good in my arms. Right. Like she belongs there. Which is why I can't stay in this bed any longer. If I do, I'm going to wake her up, fuck her, and then we'll both have to face the reality of what happened last night. I doubt she's ready for that. I know I'm not.

I slide my arm out from beneath her and climb out of bed, careful not to wake her. The sheet shifts with me, exposing her creamy skin and her perfect tits. Tits I had my hands on last night. My mouth on. I'm tempted to crawl back into bed, but it's a bad idea. This. Us. I shake my head. Her mom just died and what do I do? *Christ,* I'm a prick. I completely took advantage when she was grieving, when ... my mind wanders and I start to count the days. Shit. Shit. I cover my face with my hand. She's seventeen. *You took the girl's virginity at seventeen.*

Even I know how seriously messed up that is.

Leaving her in my bed, I opt for a cold shower. Five minutes in and my dick is still rock hard, like it knows Kasey is on the other side of the wall, naked and waiting.

I fist my cock in my hand, stroking myself to relieve the pressure, when the shower curtain is pulled back and a very awake and very naked Kasey stands before me. She sees me, sees my fingers wrapped around my cock, and steps inside the shower, dropping to her knees to replace my hand with her own.

My dick jerks at her touch and a smile curls her lips.

"Shit." What is this girl doing to me? "Kasey?" I groan. I'm not sure if it's a warning or a plea.

Her big blue eyes look up at me through her lashes, her fingers barely able to close around my length. My gaze drops to her mouth, and the image of her lips wrapping around the head of my cock has me straining painfully in her grip. It would be so easy to slip between her lips, and I know it'd feel good. A thought trickles into my mind, wondering if she's done this with another guy. Last night, I was the first to take her pussy. Would I be the first to take her mouth, too?

I want that. It's selfish and wrong, but I want all of her firsts. Everything that she'll give me.

Her tongue darts out, licking the drop of pre-cum from my slit and I thrust forward, unable to stop myself. She smiles, and it undoes something inside of me.

"You can't touch me like that, baby girl." My voice is hoarse, the tendons in my neck straining. "If you open that mouth of yours again. I'm going to take it."

I'm clearly insane, or just a glutton for punishment and high on lust, because instead of pulling away from her touch, I press forward, rubbing my dick over her mouth, enjoying the sight of my lingering pre-cum as it paints her lips.

I put one hand against the wall to steady myself, the other fists the back of her head, holding her in place, but I don't push myself inside her mouth. She has to be the one to make that decision. She shows me what she wants. What she's willing to give me.

"Have you sucked a guy's cock before?" Her eyes are dilated, filled with lust and need as she bobs her head.

I grunt. *Fuck.* I hate that answer. My grip in her hair tightens and she hisses, but doesn't try to pull away.

"You want my cock?"

Another nod.

Fuck it. I'm going to hell for this, but I was probably heading that direction anyway.

"Open your mouth, baby. Suck my cock."

She widens her stance, a telling sign that she knows what's coming and she's accepting it. Bracing herself, but not to suck on my dick. She's bracing for me to fuck her mouth.

Her lips part and like the impatient bastard I am, I thrust forward, filling her mouth until I reach the back of her throat. She doesn't gag or pull away like I expect her to. Instead, she relaxes her throat, opening her mouth wider, and takes more of me in. *"Jesus Christ!"*

Her eyes hold mine, tears leaking from the corners, but she doesn't let up. Her cheeks hollow out, sucking me harder while I pump my dick into her mouth.

"Fuck, yeah. Just like that," I throw my head back, groaning.

With both hands now, I hold the back of her head, pumping into her mouth, but it isn't enough.

A growl tears out of my throat, low and rough, my entire body tensing, but I don't want to come in her mouth right now. I want inside her cunt. I want her pussy milking my release from me, so that's what I'm going to have.

I grip her arms and jerk her to her feet. Wide eyes meet mine but I don't answer the unspoken question in them. Turning off the water I don't bother to dry off before I lift her out and set her down in front of the sink. I capture her mouth, my teeth tugging at her bottom lip. "Are you wet for me, baby?"

She moans into the kiss, her body shuddering in my arms. I slip two fingers into her, pushing in deep. She gasps against my mouth, her hands gripping my shoulders for support.

"So fucking wet," I murmur against her lips. I pull out, and instead of licking her juices from my fingers, I bring them to her mouth, pressing them between her lips. I'm transfixed, watching her mouth open, seeing her eyes shudder as she tastes herself. A small moan slips past her lips and my control shatters.

I turn her away from me to face the mirror, her eyes holding mine. Her fingers splay on the counter and I step up behind her, a firm hand on her hip, the other between her legs. Her eyes hold mine captive as I scrape my teeth over her shoulder, and I see the moment she gives herself to me.

I line my cock up with her entrance, her wet pussy coating my head when I realize I'm bare. Shit. I suck in a breath and hold myself immobile. Kasey presses herself back and I grind my teeth together, my hand on her hip the only thing keeping her in place.

"I need to grab a condom," I bite out.

Her eyes widen with understanding, but neither of us move.

"I'm on the pill," she says, voice soft. Hesitant. "I've been on it since I was sixteen. I'm good."

Thank fuck.

I nod. "I'm clean," I tell her.

"Okay."

Okay.

I press into her, watching her face for a reaction as my cock slips between her folds. She gasps, head falling back on her shoulders to expose her neck. Without even thinking, one hand slides up her body, stopping briefly to toy with one nipple, squeeze her full breasts, before wrapping around her throat in a possessive hold.

She moans and I thrust into her harder. Faster. "God, you're tight." I bite out the words as my hips pound furiously into her. I should slow down, ease her into this. She's got to be sore after last night, but I can't muster the control needed to pull back.

She presses her ass into me, meeting me thrust for thrust. My hand flexes on her throat, her cries getting louder. "Oh, god," she moans, the walls of her pussy damn near strangling my cock. Her orgasms rocks through her. She arches her back, legs shaking, and I circle her clit, drawing out her release.

When her legs buckle, I push her forward, pinning her legs between me and the counter. With a hand on her back I push her down until her cheek is pressed against the mirror, her heavy breathing fogging up the glass.

My pelvis slams against her ass, my cock nudging her cervix as I bury myself deep. She isn't even trying to hold in her needy moans, which only serve to spur me on more. Her inner muscles clench around my dick, and I drive into her hard and fast, chasing my own release and grinding against her. My balls draw up tight, muscles clenching, and with one final thrust and an agonizing groan, I'm spilling my cum inside her.

My legs shake and I pull out, Kasey still slumped on the counter. I turn the shower back on, checking the temperature to make sure it's ready before pulling her under the warm spray and washing the signs of sex from both our bodies. Neither of us speaks, but when I move to wash between her thighs, she slaps my hand away.

Right.

We don't do gentle or sweet. We fuck. She doesn't want tenderness from me.

Grabbing us each a towel we dry off and I get dressed in my room. Kasey retreats to the guest room where her clothes are and comes back a few minutes later wearing a pair of white cut-off shorts and a red top. She has a frown on her face and a determined look in her eyes.

"I have a game today," I tell her.

She nods. "You mentioned that yesterday."

"Do you want to come? Allie and Bibi will be there watching the guys. You wouldn't be alone."

She bites her bottom lip, and I have to keep myself from going to her, tugging her abused lip free only to capture it with my own teeth. She doesn't answer.

"What's going on in that head of yours?" I ask, shoving my gear in my gym bag. Between sleeping in, the shower, and the sex, I'm running late and Coach will have my ass if I don't get a move on, but something is going on in that pretty little head of hers. I need to figure it out.

"Aaron will be pissed if he finds out about this."

I grunt. "I'm aware."

"I don't want to be the reason you two have a falling out again. He needs you and the others too much."

I side eye her. "Spell it out for me, Kasey."

"You can't tell him. He can't find out about any of this." She indicates the space between us. I don't like the idea of being her dirty little secret. Not one fucking bit. But, I can't argue with her reasoning. Henderson has a lot on his plate. Me fucking his sister isn't something he needs to worry about right now. Not when me fucking his sister should never have happened in the first place, but after this morning, I can't say it won't happen again.

22

Kasey

I don't know what came over me this morning. But when I woke up and Dominique was gone, a part of me crumbled, thinking he'd left me there, alone. Then I heard the water running and I just, I needed to know this wasn't going to be like all the times before. That he wasn't going to mess around with me, only to pretend nothing ever happened.

So, I went for broke, and for once in my life, I took my shot. I pulled back the curtain, standing naked and unashamed, and when I saw him standing there with his fingers wrapped around his cock, my need reflected in his eyes, I wanted it to be my hand holding him. I wanted it to be my mouth bringing him his release.

He didn't push me away when I reached for him. He didn't tell me to stop or that he didn't want it. Want me. He moaned when I took him in my mouth. His body shuddered when he spilled his release inside me from behind.

This can't go anywhere, but I don't want to stop. I need whatever this is right now to chase away my grief. To push back the pain. I'm not stupid. I know who he is. Who I am. I'm not going to pretend that what we have is sunshine and butterflies with a happily ever after at the end of the rainbow. Because the fallout, if things take a bad turn, it isn't just the two of us who will be affected. I'm not sure what is going on with my brother, but I know it has to do with more than Mom. I can't be the reason he loses his best friend, and that's what will happen if he finds out. His protective brother streak won't allow it to be any other way.

"So we're on the same page, then?" I ask, needing the confirmation.

Dominique releases a harsh breath and rubs his hand over the back of his neck. A muscle tics in his jaw, but after a few more seconds pass, he relents. "Fine, we'll be careful. Henderson will never know I'm boning his baby sister."

I bark out a laugh. Way to be presumptuous. "You think this will happen again?"

He gives me a knowing look, his hooded gaze boring into mine. "You saying it won't?"

I manage a shrug. "Whatever we're doing here, it's casual."

"Agreed."

"This is not a relationship. We're not going to hold hands and go on dates."

He grunts.

"And no catching feelings," I tell him, as much for my own benefit as his.

"I wasn't planning on it."

"Good." I nod. "Aaron can't ever know—" he opens his mouth to interrupt but I rush on to finish, "I know. You said we'll be discreet, but I mean it. My brother can't find out about this. Not even years from now, okay? It never happened."

"Fine. Anything else?"

Nothing else comes to mind, so I shake my head.

"Okay. I have questions. I like shit to be black and white. No gray area." He sucks on his teeth, his expression letting me know he's not playing around.

"Alright. What are they?"

"You and Deacon, what's going on there?"

I shrug. "Nothing. He's nice to me. I told him at the start I was only interested in being friends. He's cool with it." Dominique scoffs, but I don't let it get to me. "Why? Because, just so we're clear, screwing my brains out doesn't mean you own me. You don't get to dictate who I talk to or who I'm friends with."

His jaw clenches and he grunts.

"Anything else you wanna know?"

"I know you think I get around"—I snort at that—"but if I'm fucking a girl more than once, she's the only girl I'm fucking, you feel me?"

I narrow my eyes. "What are you saying, exactly?"

"If you decide being *friends*," he growls, "with Deacon isn't enough for you. If you want his dick or someone else's, do me a solid and let me know before you go testing the waters, alright? I'll be sure to give you the same consideration if I find myself in a similar situation."

Anger flashes through me at the thought of him with anyone else. He sees it, and a slow smile spreads across his face.

"Deal?" he asks.

I want to wipe the smug look off his face, but manage to grit out, "Deal."

"Last question." He waits until I nod. "Do you want a relationship? Is that what you're really looking for here?" His tone is even. His eyes not meeting mine. There is zero inflection in his voice to let me know if he's asking because he wants that, or if he hates the idea and just wants to make sure I don't want one too.

I go with the response I think he's most after because right now, I need him to fuck me when I feel like I'm going to spiral and I need him not to be cagey about it. "With you? Definitely not." His eyes snap to mine, searching. "Look," I tuck my hair behind my ears and lay everything out for him.

"You're arrogant, and most of the time, I can barely stand to be in the same room as you."

"The feeling is mutual."

"Right. So, a relationship would never work between us, assuming either of us even wanted one, but fooling around I'm fine with. Does that work for you? I don't need you to beat around the bush, either. I'm not a kid whose feelings you're going to hurt with a rejection." The silence stretches between us. "It's a yes or no question," I tell him, my patience growing thin.

He releases a breath, and without answering, he pulls me into his chest and slams his mouth down on mine. His kiss is all-consuming, leaving my head spinning and my heart racing out of my chest.

A needy moan slips past my lips when he finally pulls away. Dark brown eyes meet my own, and in them I see my own desire reflected back to me. "This works for me," he says. Then he hesitates and asks, "When is your birthday? I know it's coming up, but I don't know the date."

"It was yesterday."

He pulls back, eyes wide. "You turned eighteen yesterday?" I nod. "And no one said shit? No one remembered, not even your brother?"

I shrug. "Shit happened. It's bad timing," I give him a considering look. "Or good, depending on how you look at it."

He smirks. "Yeah, I see what you're saying." He grabs his gym bag and heads for the door, pausing at the threshold to give me a backward glance. "Game's at eleven. I have to get to the field early and warm up." I nod, my lips pressing together. "Show up. I don't want you sitting here alone. You can call one of the girls for a ride if you don't want to drive yourself."

"I'll think about it," I say, and his eyes darken.

"I'll see you there. Eleven. And if you wear my number, I'll think about giving you a belated birthday gift." He gives me a heated look, and before I can respond, he's gone.

What the hell did I just get myself into?

We're just getting started with Dominique and Kasey. Their story continues in Cruel Promise. Grab your copy today!

If you're new to the series, check out Wicked Devil, book 1 in the Devils of Sun Valley High series to when sparks really started to fly with these two. It's Roman & Allie's book but Dominique and Kasey play a big part in the story! You won't want to miss it.

And if you're intrigued by Deacon, you'll want to read The Savage, book 1 in the Boys of Richland series. Deacon will eventually make a jump over here and you won't want to miss it when he does.

MISCHIEF

a devils of sun valley and boys of richland cross over story

MANAGED

Hasn't he realized ordering me not to do something just means I'm that much more determined to do it?

BONUS SHORT STORY

Mischief Managed is a short story previously featured in the **Hallowed Nights Anthology** (no longer in publication)

It takes place shortly after the ending in Cruel Devil and is through the lens of Kasey and Deacon ... yes, Deacon.

23

Kasey

G od, yes. Right there. I'm so freaking close and god do I need an orgasm right now. I'm sure everyone could use the big O bright and early each morning, but I really, really need it. Today more so than most because I am an idiot. I deleted my voicemail inbox. Just wiped the entire stupid thing clean without even registering what I was doing.

Tears prick the backs of my eyes as I think about Mom's last message. Her voice. The fact that I'll never hear it again. It was such a dumb mistake and I hate myself for not paying better attention. For letting my grief and sleep deprivation get the better of me because now I'll never have that message back. I tried. For over an hour, I fought with my stupid phone. I Googled all the ideas. None of it worked.

I blink hard, determined to clear my vision. I'm having sex for chrissakes. Now is not the time to fall apart.

Come on, Kasey. Focus on Dominique. That's why I came over here in the first place. The grief crept in and I needed a dose of dopamine to chase my blues away.

I have a problem. One I am very well aware of and have absolutely zero intention of correcting. At least, not anytime soon. Because it works. It's the only thing that's worked and trust me, I've tried all the things. Drinking away my sorrows—which is more difficult than it should be as an eighteen-year-old college student.

Getting in fights. That one went well. I almost got kicked out of my sorority house, earned myself a black eye, and had not one, but two, hour long lectures, between Dominique and my brother, about how reckless and immature I'd been and how disappointed they were in me. I shouldn't care what they think of me, but pulling the disappointed card fucking hurt.

After that I tried a little weed, but that didn't work out too well, either. I learned, though, that weed is not for me. I think it was mixed with something, or maybe it was a weird strain. I'm not sure. But I hallucinated some shit and wound up even more messed up than I was before.

My bad.

Quinn my Big at Kappa Mu said I kept calling out for my dead mother. So yeah, I won't be trying that again.

But this... sex? It works.

Every time I get in my head, or the grief creeps a little too close, I chase this right here. This feeling of being owned.

Claimed. Of his skin on mine and pleasure coursing through my veins. It's the best high out there.

My heart races, my throat already hoarse from moaning and crying out Dominique's name. I showed up on his doorstep fifteen minutes ago having rolled out of bed, looking like hell with messy hair and red-rimmed eyes and Dominique took one look at me, ushered me inside, and the next thing I knew he had me bent me over the dining table and was fucking me from behind, chasing all of my pain away.

Sex is the cure-all for everything but cancer, if you ask me.

And death. It definitely cannot fix death. But anything else — My mind hooks onto that thought. Of dying. Of losing the people you love. Not getting to say goodbye. Suddenly, the sound of tires screeching fills my ears like a roar, and her screams rattle through my skull. Metal crunches.

I close my eyes. *Deep breaths, Kasey.*

This is not where I want my head to be right now.

I swallow the lump in my throat. *Breathe. In and out. Come on. Fucking breathe. You've got this.* I repeat the words in my head. Over and over but... Urgh!

Come. On.

Fuck.

I focus on the feel of Dominique inside me. Of his hands digging into my hips, fingers biting into my flesh. There will be bruises tomorrow, but I don't care. I relish every mark he leaves on my body, and I admire them everytime I need to remind myself of what this feels like. Of how it can make everything else wash away. My breath catches in my throat and I'm overwhelmed by the feeling of his powerful body curling over mine, wrapping me in his heat and his strength. His chest brushes along my back and I shiver beneath him, sucking in another lungful of air.

That's it. Right there. Focus on the good. Another deep breath, in through my nose and out through my mouth.

Don't think about Mom. Think about sex. Think about getting right... there.

I score my finger-tips along the table's edge and my toes curl as I chase my release. So fucking close, if I can just keep my mind in the gutter where it belongs...

I push my hips back and take Dom deeper, clenching my teeth against the sharp spear of pain because he's big, and this angle, it's a lot to take. But as he pounds in and out of me, whatever discomfort I'm feeling is washed away and replaced by a pleasure so intense that spots flicker behind my eyes.

Dominique's hand tangles in my blond curls before he pulls back, forcing my gaze up. I shiver again, swallowing past my emotions. My back arches, the tendons in my neck straining as my body contorts to his will.

I snap my eyes open, but my gaze is unseeing, lost in the haze of lust and want and need.

"You like that?" he growls, his warm breath washing over the shell of my ear.

He's close too and I fucking love it. When he gets like this, rough and dominant and... "Fuck, yes," I hiss.

The sound of flesh against flesh fills the room. This has become a habit the past few months. Him in my room or me in his. We fight. We fuck. Rinse and repeat.

I'm grateful for it. I might despise Dominique ninety percent of the time, but that ten percent when he's buried deep inside me, I actually like the smug bastard.

I crave him. Would give my left tit to have him. Just like this. Every night. And every morning.

Which is why this is so dangerous.

He's Dominique Price for god's sake, and I cannot afford to get hooked on him. Star football player and asshole extraordinaire. He's the starting quarterback for Suncrest U, on the path to NFL stardom, and he's been best friends with my older brother Aaron since they were kids. Now that they're both in college, they live together. Rent this townhouse like two peas in a pod. Proverbial BFFs.

But despite all that, we both know this is one relationship my brother will never approve of, and one I know, without a shadow of a doubt, would never work between us anyway, even if he did. Assuming I actually wanted a relationship with Dominique Price.

Which, for the record, I don't.

And he doesn't want one with me either. We barely get along. If it wasn't for our friends, we wouldn't talk to one another, let alone force ourselves to be civil.

Okay, we're not even that. But I mean, sometimes I try.

It doesn't matter though. None of it does.

I need Dominique Price. I hate to admit it, but it's the truth.

I've gotten more and more reckless as the weeks have passed. And if I don't shape up and start being careful, we're going to get caught. And screwing like this, a whopping twenty feet from the front door, is just plain stupid.

I know this. He knows this.

Did that stop either of us from doing it, anyway?

At the moment, I'm bent over a table with my leggings still hanging off one leg and my ass up in the air, in their kitchen no less, with Dominique pounding into me so... obviously not.

I might be addicted to his dick.

But given that it took him a matter of minutes to get me partially undressed before he was thrusting inside me, I'd say he is equally addicted to my pussy.

Knowing this shouldn't bring a smile to my face. He's an asshole. A Grade A, domineering, arrogant, possessive, asshole.

But God does being bent over by him feel good. It's freaking great, actually.

Which ladies and gentlemen, is why I have a problem. Because I cannot afford to be addicted to Dominique's dick. I mentioned that, right? If I allow this to continue, there is a very good chance I'll get hooked on the person attached to said dick. And that cannot happen.

He'd be easier to quit if the sex was bad. Hell, I could walk away from mediocre, or decent, even. But this— this all-consuming, fucking amazing, screw-me-mindless sex, is impossible to quit. And even though I realize I have nothing to compare it to, given that I slipped Dominique my V-card in a moment of grief induced insanity, there is no way it can get any better than this.

No fucking way.

We've been sneaking around to sleep with each other for weeks now. It's never dull. He's always amazing. I get off every single time. And I swear I always want more. I expected the newness of it all to eventually wear off. For this... craving to go away. But it doesn't. Dominique Price is like tequila to an alcoholic, and a shot of him goes down so damn smooth.

The sex has been an almost every day—or at the very least, every other day—occurrence since we started this up. But football season is well underway, and of course Suncrest U is killing it.

Dominique's time has been limited this week, more so than most. Between training in the mornings, classes in the afternoons, then practice after school and games every weekend, half of which require travel, we barely see each other.

I'm exhausted for him just thinking about his schedule. Not that he'll get any sympathy from me. That's not how this little arrangement works. He scratches my back. I scratch his. And we both satisfy an itch the other has. But lately, something's felt off. Like there's something missing, but I don't know what.

I've tried to ignore the feeling which is easier to do on days like today. When I remember that less than eight weeks ago, my mom died in a tragic car accident. That she was in the middle of leaving me a message when she crashed and that I'd been too busy ignoring her to answer. And now it's gone. Her message is gone. Her voice. The words she spoke, telling me she loved me. It's all fucking gone. And god dammit. Here I go again. What is wrong with me?

I suck in a ragged breath and Dominique's thrusts slow.

This is why I'm here right now. Why I showed up on his doorstep barely after seven AM. Because of that stupid voicemail. It haunts me.

Dominique curses, drawing my attention back to him. He releases his hold on my hair and spins me around to face him. His dick slides out of me with the change in position and a noise not unlike a sob passes over my lips.

"I've got you," he says, and he lifts me onto the edge of the table, spreading my thighs open for him to step between.

Wrapping my legs around his waist, I let out a small sigh of relief as he thrusts back into me. I throw my head back, more than ready for this to continue, and brace myself against the table, expecting Dominique to fuck me hard like he'd been doing only seconds before, except he doesn't. In fact, he does the complete opposite.

Cupping the nape of my neck, he tilts my head forward until he's all that I see. Dark brown eyes framed with heavy brows meet my baby blue gaze and he sinks into me almost painfully slow. I take in the hard lines of his face. The twin slashes that cut thin lines into his brow and his dark brown skin. He's the same arrogant asshole he's always been only now, he looks at me like I'm more than his best friend's little sister. Like I'm more than an easy lay.

His dark brown eyes are soft, gaze heavy lidded. He peppers my face with tender kisses, his lips brushing along my cheeks, my nose, and trailing down along my neck before making their way to my lips and covering my mouth with his. He swallows my sounds of protest and his hand cups the side of my neck, holding me in place but also supporting me with his strength.

Dominique pulls out until only the tip of him is still inside me before sinking into me again. Slow. Methodical. Eyes boring into mine and making the act that much more intense.

It's... intimate.

I don't like it.

His gaze searches mine for something. It's like he's asking me a question, but I can't make out the words to give him a response. His hands roam over my body, skimming over my ribs. He peels my shirt up, exposing my stomach and chest as he tugs down the cup of my bra and palms one of my breasts in his large hands. He rolls my nipple between his thumb and forefinger while I'm struggling to increase our pace.

I dig my heels into his lower back, encouraging him to go faster. To thrust into me harder. But he refuses to budge. With a grimace, he controls himself, thrusting in and out of me at a measured pace, never giving me what I need. Keeping it slow and steady, like he's worried I might break. Or worse. Fucking shatter.

"How's that, baby girl?" His voice rasps over my heated skin as he touches his forehead to mind.

"Fuck me," I snarl and he chuckles, shaking his head.

His thumb grazes my lower lip, and he leans in like he's about to kiss me again, only to whisper a single word against my mouth. "No."

I groan and move to shove him away from me, but pushing Dominique is like trying to move a mountain. "You want me to stop?" he asks, surprise coloring his voice.

"No," I snap. "I want you to fuck me like you hate me. Give me what I need, Dom."

I cringe, hearing the whine in my voice, but thankfully, Dominique doesn't pick up on it. But neither does he do what I ask.

"You can't tell me this doesn't feel good," he demands, continuing to thrust in and out of me. I look down at where our bodies connect, watching his smooth, dark shaft sink into me, and without meaning to, I release another breathy moan.

The sight of his dick does things to me I can't even explain. He has a beautiful dick. Long and thick. He's perfectly symmetrical, the skin smooth and just a few shades lighter at the tip. His hand dips between us, practiced fingers finding my clit.

"I feel that sweet pussy of yours clenching around my cock. You want this. Don't pretend you don't." Keeping with his slow pace, he thrusts into me a little harder, not giving me the friction I want but hitting a deeper point inside of me that has me digging my fingers into his flesh, holding on to his biceps like I need him to anchor me, like I'm worried he'll leave if I don't.

"Fuck." He hits that spot deep inside me, the perfect one that lets me know my release is in sight. His callused fingers strum my clit, increasing the pleasure tenfold. "Harder," I demand.

"No."

"Faster, then."

He nips at my bottom lip.

"No."

"Screw you, Dominique. Fuck me."

His eyes flash with pure lust, and his lips curve into a cruel smile. "What do you think we're doing here, baby girl?"

Sweat drips down my hairline, my chest rising and falling rapidly as I fight to slow my heart rate. Meanwhile, he continues to rub teasing circles around my clit. "Oh God."

"That's it, baby girl. Let go. I've got you," he murmurs, his voice softer than I've ever heard it.

My muscles tense and my eyes flutter closed. A whimper passes over my lips as intense waves build inside me. He's too good at this. No one should be this good at sex.

The hand at my throat tightens, not enough to restrict my airway, but just enough to add a spike of adrenaline to my system, and then I'm flying. My pussy clenches around him as wave after wave of pleasure skates through my entire body. I slump back, my spine meeting the cool wood of the table as Dominique milks out every ounce of my release, leaving me boneless.

Fuck, that was... amazing.

He looms over me, bracing himself on either side of me as he continues to thrust in and out of me, and then his lips are on mine and his hot cum is filling me as he shudders through his own release.

He pulls back enough to meet my eyes. His mouth opens to say what, I'm not sure, because the next thing I know there are familiar voices outside and Dominique is cursing, sliding out of me as I rush to slip my legs back into my leggings and right my top.

I jump down from the table, panic rushing through me.

"Kasey..."

"Get dressed," I hiss.

His cum leaks out of my center, but I don't have time to deal with that right now because I'm almost positive Bibiana and Allie are about to walk in right now. I pull the hair tie from my wrist and throw my hair into the fastest messy bun I can manage just as there's a knock at the door, followed by it opening and my two best friends coming inside.

"Hey!" Allie calls.

"Kasey, we went by the Kappa Mu house and Quinn said we'd find you here. Are you kicking it with Aaron today? How's he doing?" Bibiana asks, waddling further into the house. She's close to eight months pregnant now and looks ready to pop. It'd be cute if I didn't know just how miserable she is. The beginning of the pregnancy went well enough, but she's struggling this last trimester. She's tired and sore and from what I've gathered, more than ready for baby Chavez to make his debut.

I hook my thumb behind me and snort. "I was trying to, but all I found was this ray of sunshine." Bibiana gives me a knowing smirk. One I choose to ignore, and claims one of the dining chairs, carefully lowering herself into it, one hand holding her round belly.

"Hey Dom." She exhales a sigh of relief and he gives her a quick kiss on the cheek before moving to grab the giant box in Allie's arms.

"What's all this for?" he asks her.

Allie gives him a mischievous smirk. "We bought forks. It's the day before Halloween and we're going forking."

Dominique drops the box on the table, giving me a heated look while the girls are distracted. One that clearly says he'd like to do some forking, too.

I roll my eyes and a smug look curls the corners of his mouth, so I flip him off and turn my attention to the girls.

"What the hell is forking?"

Allie opens the box and shows us the contents inside. Hundreds of plastic forks greet me. "I'm glad you ask," she says, holding one up. "Forking is when you take a bunch of plastic forks and stab them into the grass. Usually you do this to someone's yard but today we're going to go fork PacNorth's soccer field."

My brows pull together. "Why are we forking their field?" Not that I'm against it. Just curious what brought all of this on.

Her eyes flash. "Because Julio is a butthead."

Bibiana snickers.

Julio is Allie's best friend from her hometown and if she's upset with him, he must have messed up royally because last I checked, in Allie's mind, Julio damn near walks on water.

I grab a fork from the box and hold it out to Allie. "This one is a spork."

She grabs it from me and tosses it back into the box. "I bought all the forks at Pauli's Grocer and sporks were the next best thing. Spoons don't really work."

"What's the point of this?" Dominique asks. "Sticking forks in a university field doesn't seem very effective if you're trying to make a point, here."

Allie huffs out a breath. "Maybe we should fork your field," she mutters.

"Game. Anytime," I tell her, and offer her a high five.

Dominique glowers at us, but we all ignore it. He loves Allie and Bibi as though they're his sisters and they know it, so his scary face doesn't work on them and me. I like seeing his angry face. It means I managed to piss him off, which happens to be my second favorite pastime lately. After the screwing, that is.

"You stick the fork in the field. And when the offending party goes to yank them out. They snap." She breaks one for added effect. "It's annoying as hell and makes unforking the field tedious and annoying. Julio hates stupid shit like this, so it's the perfect kind of revenge."

"Revenge for what, exactly?" I ask. Julio is Allie's bestie from her home town and as far as I knew, the man could do no wrong.

"He got drunk and made out with Adrianna."

I suck in a breath.

"The chick who fucked your ex before he was your ex?"

"Yep. She was Allie's best girl friend at the time, too," Bibiana adds, and I wince. That's a serious girl code violation.

Dominique whistles and steps back from the table. "This sounds like a good time for me to head out. You ladies have fun forking or whatever you want to call it."

"What? No!" Allie whines. "We need a getaway driver. That's you!"

Dominique shakes his head. "Can't. I'm training with the boys today."

She mutters out a curse and smacks her palm over her face. "I knew that. Roman was talking about it last night. I don't know how that slipped my mind." She pauses. "Well crap. Who's going to be our getaway driver now?"

"Why don't you want to drive? You've got the Audi," I remind her.

She gives me the *'please tell you're kidding'* look. "Richland is two hours away." As if that answers the question. "I do not want to have to watch the boring ass road for two hours while you bitches get to relax in your seats." Okay, fair point. I don't want to make that drive either. Being a passenger will be bad enough. There's nothing but farmland between here and Richland, so you can't even take in the view because there just isn't one.

"And I'm pregnant," Bibi adds.

"I think we're all very much aware of that."

She rolls her eyes. "Yeah, yeah. But I'm a shit driver and my stomach bumps into the steering wheel every time I try to go anywhere."

I pull out my phone and go with the phone a friend option. If I don't, then I'm ninety-five percent positive it'll be me stuck as the driver and yeah, no thanks. I turn it on speaker phone, knowing this will get a reaction and feeling entirely okay with that.

Dominique turns to head out of the room, not even bothering to say bye, not that any of us are surprised. He's not much of a talker, that one. But before he's made it far, the call connects and Deacon's voice chimes out of my phone.

"Hey. What's up?"

Dominique's entire body stiffens.

"Hey. The girls and I are heading to Richland to play a prank on some friends. We need a getaway driver. You in?"

He doesn't even hesitate. "I'm down. My schedule's clear since Coach is doing some bullshit training exercise with the starting line players today. When are we heading out?"

Before I can answer, Dominique tears the phone from my hand and ends the call. "No." He barks out.

Silence fills the room.

I glare at him and hold my hand out for my phone.

"Kasey—" there's a warning in his voice. One I choose to ignore.

"I thought you needed to go to training?" I ask.

His nostrils flare. "Deacon is bad news. Find someone else or fuck, don't go at all. But you are not spending the day with that asshole."

He's funny if he thinks that's going to stop me. Hasn't he realized ordering me not to do something just means I'm that much more determined to do it?

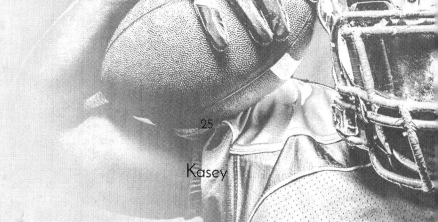

25

Kasey

Twenty minutes and a good fight with Dominique later and we're piling into Deacon's car and heading to Richland to fork the soccer field. Allie is giddy with excitement, but I imagine that'll fade soon. PacNorth is a two-hour drive away, so I settle in for our mini road trip and play with the stereo until I find a station I like. Sueco's *Paralyzed* plays over the speakers and I lean back, letting the music shake loose some of my lingering tension. The argument with Dominique would have gone on longer if it wasn't for the fact he couldn't be late to practice, but when he finally stormed out of the house, I called Deacon back and he was immediately down.

"You owe me," Deacon reminds me.

I roll my eyes and turn to look at him. He keeps his eyes on the road but reaches out and gives me a light shove on the shoulder.

"Pretty sure you owe me for getting Dominique off your ass."

He grunts. "Pretty sure Dominique was only ever on my ass because of you."

He's not wrong. But that's not really my fault either. It's his.

"How much are we betting that this puts me firmly back on his shit list?" he asks, not sounding at all worried. It's stupid really. I mean, I'm glad he agreed to take us. Allie was right. Being stuck in the driver's seat would have sucked. But he knew what he was doing when he agreed. Dominique's gone all big brother over me on his ass before. So have Roman and Emilio, for that matter. And he still agreed to come, so that's on him.

I release an exaggerated sigh. "Ah, the consequences of our actions. Don't you just hate when they strike?"

"What's this about Dominique?" Allie pipes up from the backseat.

"Nothing. Just that he's an asshole," I tell her, a smile in my voice.

"Truth," Deacon mutters and gives me a fist bump in solidarity. Dominique might not be kicking his ass on the field anymore, but those two will never be friends. Dom's inner circle is tight and given the rocky start these two had, it'll be a long day in hell before they ever have anything close to a civilized conversation with each other. A fact which Dominique could give two shits about. He's not looking to make friends. Though Deacon's a nice, personable guy, I wonder if it bothers him how much Dominique dislikes him?

"Dominique is one of the sweetest guys I know," Allie argues. "How you manage to pull the worst out of him always surprises me."

"He really is incredibly sweet. He used to watch Luis for me and Emilio during his non-schedule back at Sun Valley High, remember? That man has a heart of gold," Bibiana adds.

I snort. "He's sweet to you two. To us," I indicate the space between Deacon and I, "he's an asshole. Always has been. I'm his friend's annoying little sister—"

"And I'm the guy gunning for his spot on the field," Deacon finishes.

Allie reaches forward and pats him on the arm. "Hate to break it to you, but until he graduates, you can go after it all you want, but it's not going to happen. Coach will never replace Dominique as the starting QB, and with the way things are looking, he's going to land the Heisman. Again."

Deacon huffs out a breath. "I'm aware. Doesn't mean he doesn't still hate me."

Now it's Bibi's turn to roll her eyes. "Doubt it. He probably doesn't ever think of you." She touches her forefinger to her lower lip. "Though now that I think about it, when Kasey called you to drive us, he did look two seconds away from committing murder. What was that about, anyway?"

"I've always said there's something going on between these two. Maybe he doesn't like the idea of another guy near Kasey." Allie says it flippantly, but in the back of my mind, I'm silently freaking out. If Allie and Bibiana figure out what we're doing, then their significant others—Roman and Emilio —will know too. And if they find out, no way will Aaron not get wind of it. I need to shove them off that trail of thought right away.

"Hardly," I chuckle. "He just likes to play the protective older brother part whenever Aaron isn't around. I've heard him call it some bro code bullshit or something. I wouldn't read too much into it."

Deacon gives me the side eye but thankfully says nothing and after a few comments from the girls about what a bummer that is, and how it would have been so great if we got along and coupled up like they did, I finally get them onto the topic of Bibi's impending birth and get sucked into talks about her birthing plan and the baby shower, and all things baby Chavez.

Thank god for that. They don't really need much input from me, so I relax while they talk about themes and colors, whether Bibiana wants a doula or if she just wants Emilio in the room when the baby comes.

Deacon doesn't join the discussion. Instead, he pulls out his phone, typing a quick, one-handed message before tossing it in the car's cup holder.

My phone vibrates in my pocket and I frown at him as I pull it out, Deacon's name flashing across the screen.

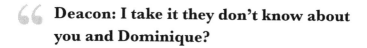 **Deacon: I take it they don't know about you and Dominique?**

I scowl at him and type out a response.

Me: There's nothing to know.

His phone chirps and he reads my message, grunts, and types out a reply.

Deacon: Bullshit. You two fucked in the locker room last week.

I turn wide eyes toward him. Floored. I am fucking floored right now. He saw us? We checked and double checked that no one was in there. How the hell could he—Another message comes in.

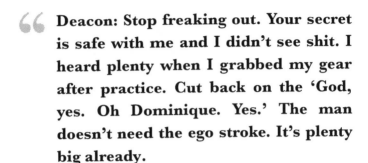

> **Deacon: Stop freaking out. Your secret is safe with me and I didn't see shit. I heard plenty when I grabbed my gear after practice. Cut back on the 'God, yes. Oh Dominique. Yes.' The man doesn't need the ego stroke. It's plenty big already.**

I cover my face with my hand, heat rising in my cheeks. He knows. Shit. No one is supposed to know.

"You okay?" Bibi asks.

I give her a thumbs up, keeping my face turned away from her as my mind scrambles to come up with an excuse. A way to deny this, but I've got nothing. Literally nothing. "Yep. Super peachy."

Deacon, for his part, laughs and I know with that sound alone that, while he might not tell—jury is out on that though because I don't know him that well — he definitely plans to use this against me. *Great.*

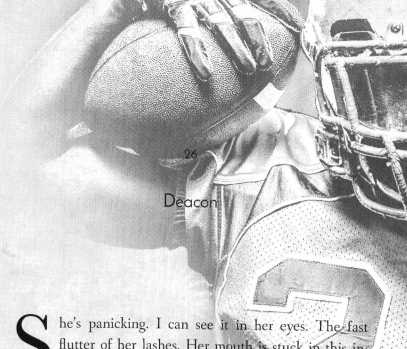

26

Deacon

She's panicking. I can see it in her eyes. The fast flutter of her lashes. Her mouth is stuck in this in-between stage with her lips parted like she wants to speak but has no idea what to say. It's fucking cute as shit. No wonder Price wants her all for himself.

Too bad the fucker can't always have what he wants. He has shit so fucking easy. Life given to him on a silver platter. And if I can't take his spot on the team, then I've got no issue swooping in and claiming his girl as my consolation prize instead.

Don't get me wrong. He's earned his stripes. I won't deny that. Right now, he's the better quarterback. But he's not the better man. Sooner or later, Kasey is going to realize that.

I slide my hand over the center console and give her knee a squeeze. "Relax. I've got you," I tell her. I could fuck Price over with this information if I wanted to. There's a reason he and Kasey are keeping things on the down low. I don't know what they are yet. But I'll find out. And in the meantime, I'll hang on to this knowledge, earn Kasey's trust, and show her why she's wasting her time with a dude who's clearly uninterested in showing her off. *Idiot.* It's like he has no clue what a fucking catch she is. She's younger than him by a few years so it could be that but I can't imagine that's reason enough to avoid laying a public claim on the girl.

She swallows hard, her throat bobbing with the motion, and I leave my hand on her knee for the rest of the drive. I'm not sure if she realizes it's there, likes that I'm touching her, or is just too lost in that pretty head of hers to care.

Either one works for me. I've spent the last few weeks building a relationship with this chick and doing my damnedest to not get stuck in the friend zone, which is a hell of a lot harder than I expected.

I'm an alright looking guy. Getting a girl's attention has never been an issue. But Kasey isn't like other girls. She's feisty and could give two shits what anyone thinks about her, and she never has a problem speaking her mind.

I've managed to make touches like this casual. Normal and to be expected.

She doesn't bat an eye anymore when I toss my arm around her shoulder and walk with her after class, or when I pull her in for a quick hug goodbye. She's comfortable with me. And Price fucking hates it. Knowing that it eats away at him is the only thing keeping me sane these days.

Tuition bills are racking up and if I can't move up to a starting position, my parents aren't going to help with tuition any longer. My pops says if you're not the best then you're wasting your time but I love competing. I was born to play. I'm fast as shit, have quick reflexes, and I'm solid under pressure. No way am I going to let a guy like Dominique Price get in the way of my future. I might not be the best yet, but I can be. He just needs to be knocked off his game.

The drive goes by quickly, the girls talking about babies and all the things I have zero clue about, but it keeps them busy and lets me clear my thoughts before we're pulling up to PacNorth University. Allie directs me to the soccer field and I park at the rear, away from the rest of the cars in the lot. What she's planning seems harmless enough but the girls want to be sneaky and shit, like this is some big covert operation.

We all get out of the car and I keep an eye on the pregnant one. Bibiana. I know she's Emilio's chick and obviously very pregnant. On the drive, I overheard her saying she still has a ways to go but no way can the girl get any bigger. She's small. Over a foot shorter than me and all belly. If I didn't know for a fact she was carrying E's kid, I'd assume she shoved a basketball under her shirt. It's that ridiculous.

With one hand supporting her swollen stomach, she follows Allie and Kasey out of the car and to the field. I take up the rear after claiming the box of forks from Allie's grasp and scan the parking lot for anyone who might snitch on us.

"Thanks," Allie mutters, but I just nod.

My parents and I have a lot of differences, but my momma raised me right. I'm not gonna make a girl shoulder this thing when my arms are free and I'm more than capable.

"No problem. So... what's the plan?"

Allie pulls the hood of her sweatshirt up over her head. "Since it's a Saturday and the day before Halloween, the field should be empty. Everyone is off getting ready for whatever campus parties are happening tonight and tomorrow." Makes sense. "So the plan is to pretend we're supposed to be here."

"Is that why we're doing this in the middle of the day?" Kasey asks.

"Yeah. If we tried to do it at night and someone saw us, they'd immediately assume we didn't belong but since the only people who know what's going on with the field are the players and the coaches, all of whom should be gone already for the day, we should be in the clear. We might get a few curious looks but no one is going to freak out seeing us."

I tug on the back of her hood. "So what's with the cover up, then?"

She rolls her eyes. "Habit. Come on." We rush across the lot and slip through the gate onto the field and I set down the box. Allie immediately starts laying forks out on the grass in some sort of design."

"What are you doing?" Kasey asks, saving me the trouble.

"We don't have enough forks to actually fork the entire field so we're gonna spell out a message."

"What's the message?"

"Tu madre, traidor."

"Which means?"

It's Bibiana who answers. "Your momma, you traitor. It's some weird inside thing between Allie and Julio that none of us understand."

Allie smirks. "You don't need to. Just help me spell out the words. Deacon, you should probably play look out. I don't think we can really get in trouble for a harmless prank but you're an athlete and PacNorth is technically a rival school. If we get caught, I don't want to be responsible for you getting a suspension."

I nod. "Sounds good. I'll kick it by the locker rooms since that's where coaches or players are bound to head if any show up." I leave the girls to their work, scrolling through social media posts on my phone. There are a few parties going down tonight back on campus I might check out when we get back. I'm not really into Halloween and dressing up. It's never been my thing. But I don't mind when the girls go full on Slutober and display all the goods. It's like Halloween is a free pass to wear the least amount of clothing and not be crucified for it. Something you will never hear me complain about.

27

Deacon

It takes the girls over an hour to fork the field and I've blown through all my emails, looked at all the stupid videos on social media, and posted a few images to my Insta feed. Safe to say, I am bored as fuck. But they're having a blast. Bibiana is scooting across the field in a makeshift crab walk so she doesn't have to bend over, and Allie and Kasey are laughing and smiling, talking about who knows what, but it's a good look on them both.

Kasey hasn't smiled much lately. This is good for her. I heard the rumors that her mom passed, and she's had a dark cloud following her these past few weeks, so seeing her be herself again, it's good.

The click of heels on pavement draws my attention and I turn to see who it is only to do a double take. *Holy sh—.* My mouth drops open as I take in the woman walking toward me. She's digging in the oversized bag slung over her shoulder, her gaze directed down and a small furrow between her brows. She hasn't spotted me, but me and every other person—men and women alike—that she walks past, sure as hell spot her.

Wearing white skinny jeans, a low-cut sleeveless silk blouse, and strappy sandals with a small heel, she walks down the pathway like it's a runway made just for her. Her hair is natural, an afro of loose corkscrew curls that billow out around her. Shorter curls hang down in front of her face, almost like bangs. She owns her beauty. Standing out amongst everyone she passes like she doesn't care that she doesn't belong. She's not looking to fit in. She's showing everyone why they wish they were her and could stand out.

She has smooth, dark bronze skin, full plump lips, and dark brown eyes that, even from here, I know I could get fucking lost in.

"Fuck me," I mutter.

She's almost to me and it's obvious she's heading toward the field. Something I can't let happen now that the girls are wrapping up. I'm the look out. No way can I fuck this up when we're so close to the finish line.

I step away from the alcove I've been chilling in and she's forced to come to a halt. She doesn't acknowledge me for the first few seconds. Still digging through her bag until she manages to pull out her phone, which I assume is what she'd been after. She studies me, brushing a coil out of her face.

"Can I help you?" she asks. Her tone is brusque. She gives me a lightning fast once-over, and though I see a flash of interest in her gaze, she masks it and gives me an '*I'm not impressed.*' look.

"Yeah, actually." I let my gaze track over her and let my interest show. "I was hoping you'd be down for grabbing a drink with me later." I shoot my shot, knowing she'll reject it but that's alright. I'm stalling for time here.

"Sorry. I don't date students."

Well, hello there. That means she's faculty or a teacher's aide. Maybe a graduate student who helps after classes. My bet is on teachers's aide. She can't be older than twenty-five, and she doesn't seem the type to sit behind a desk all day in one of the admissions offices.

She moves to step around me, but I sidestep, keeping in her way. She makes an irritated sound and props one hand on her hip. "That's good because I'm not a student."

Her eyes widen before narrowing in doubt. "You don't go to PacNorth?"

I shake my head and step closer to her. Her breath catches, pupils dilating and yeah, she's interested.

"Nah. I just gave a friend a lift. They have a buddy who attends, so we were dropping in to say hello."

She licks her lips and gives me another once over, this one slower. Like the realization that I'm not a student grants her permission to check me out.

"I'm Deacon."

She hesitates before giving me her name. "Jameia."

Jameia. I like it. It's different. Exotic. Like her.

The phone in her hand rings and she tears her gaze from mine to answer it, flicking her eyes up once before she turns her back on me in search of some small measure of privacy.

"Hello?"

I chance a look over my shoulder as she talks to whoever her caller is. Kasey lifts her head at the same time and grimaces, getting the other girls' attention and telling them to hurry the fuck up. Allie rushes the box that'd held the plastic forks to a nearby recycling bin right as Jameia finishes her call and turns back to me.

"It was nice meeting you, Deacon. But I have an appointment to get to."

"Let me walk you," I tell her, falling into step beside her, and we head right for Kasey and the others.

"That's really okay. I'm just going to the soccer field."

I push my hands in my pockets and shrug. "I'm happy to. Besides, I'm heading out soon anyway and I'm parked over there." I indicate the lot and she nods, not having an excuse to send me away. When we get closer to the field, she realizes something is wrong and her footsteps speed up.

"You have got to be kidding me," she curses. I hide my smirk and follow a few steps behind her as she practically runs to the field. "Who did this?"

Before I can answer, not that she was really asking me, more curses fill the air and I turn to spot three Hispanic guys heading our way. "What the fuck happened?" One asks as soon as he's close. He's got tattoos running down his arms. Large roses inked over the top of his hands. His neck is covered in more ink, some colorful card design painting the columns of his throat. The work is solid, the colors vivid and bright.

He gives me a nod in greeting but turns his attention to Jameia, the others closing in around him. "I don't know. I just got here, and it was like this." She waves at the soccer field behind her and I take a few measure steps back. Now is a good time to make my getaway so after I've gone a few steps, I do a quick turn around and head for my car. Kasey's eyes are wide as they look out at me through the windshield and Allie stands beside the back rear door, her eyes bright and her smile wide.

I chuckle. Someone is obviously pleased with themselves.

I'm almost to my car when someone shouts, "Alejandra, get that fine ass of yours over here!"

I turn just as the same three guys who were talking to Jameia run my way. Hell nah.

I'm almost to my car, so I turn to face them and bark out a quick "Get in the car," to Allie. Does she listen? Of course not. Not that I'd expect anything less from one of Kasey's friends. Birds of a feather and all that shit. I hold my hands out in front of me and block their way. "Woah. Woah. Let's relax here for a minute. You three look like you have some business to handle over there," I wave toward the field. "And me and my friends have someplace to be. You'll have to catch your girl later."

Later like when her footballer boyfriend can deal with the hostility coming off him.

"Nah. I'll catch her now. Thanks man."

He shifts to pass me but I shoulder check him and he whirls on me, eyes narrowed and nostrils flaring. "We have a problem, man?" he asks.

His two friends close in and I catch sight of Jameia on the sideline, face pinched in worry, but whether for me or the others, I'm not sure.

"Yeah. We do. Allie's with me and no way am I gonna let some hot head asshole come at her the way you are right now."

He throws his head back and laughs, the other two following suit before he shakes his head and looks over my shoulder at the girl in question. "Alejandra, come out, come out wherever you are. Time to face the music, bebita. Or should I call Rome and tell him you're making friends."

She curses and I hear her storming up the sidewalk behind me. "Don't you dare, Julio. You know how jealous he can get.

Julio smirks. "Yeah. I do." He pulls out his phone and snaps a quick photo of Allie beside me. "Which is why I'mma make sure I've got evidence to back up my claim." She curses and lunges for his phone, but he holds it up in the air with a laugh, playing keep away from her. I frown, not entirely sure what I'm supposed to do here, when the car doors close behind me and Kasey and Bibiana join us.

"Delete the picture and don't be a butt head," Allie tells him. "You're already on my shit list for what you did."

Julio groans. "It was an accident."

"How exactly do you accidentally shove your tongue down my ex-best friend's throat? Hmm?"

One of the other guys steps forward. "It's not what you think, Allie. Adriana took advantage. Kissed him at a party, and when he realized who he was making out with, he pushed her away. Julio would never mess with her. You know that."

She folds her arms over her chest and huffs. "Fine. You're forgiven."

Julio's face breaks into a smile and he whoops before swooping in and throwing Allie over his shoulder. "Julio!" she cries out, and he smacks the back of her thighs. "Appreciate the forgiveness but now it's your turn to repent for your sins."

She squirms in his arms and he chuckles, carrying her like she weighs nothing. "I didn't sin!" she swears, but none of them are buying it.

Julio turns to me, Allie still slung over his shoulder, and holds a hand out. "I'm Julio, by the way. This is Gabe. Felix." He nods to the two boys beside him. "And it looks like you already met Meme."

"Meme?" I ask, looking her way. Her cheeks flush, the skin darkening.

"It's a nickname," she stammers.

I cover my laugh with a cough. "I like it." She bites her bottom lip and I turn back to Julio. "I'm Deacon. Kasey's friend."

"Ah..." He draws out the word. "So that's how these three rebels roped you into their prank."

I shrug. "You have any luck turning them down when they want something?"

He laughs at that. "I do not. Fair point. But we've still got a problem."

I raise a single brow. "How do you figure?"

"You see, I've got a game tomorrow, and a field filled with plastic utensils." He pats the back of Allie's thigh again. "And don't think I missed what you wrote there, Allie girl."

"I have no idea what you're talking about."

Julio huffs out an exasperated breath. "No? If that wasn't you, what brings you to town?" She squirms in his hold and he finally releases her, carefully dropping her to the ground.

She glares at him. Not that it does her any good. Then she turns to me and says, "Deacon wanted to check out the school. See what your football team looks like."

"Really?" Felix asks, not convinced in the slightest, but I back up Allie's lie.

"Yeah, man. I'm not so sure Suncrest U is a good fit. Figured I'd see what PacNorth had to offer."

"For fútbol?" he clarifies putting emphasis on the u.

"Uh, yeah."

Gabe chuckles and shares a look with the other two, some silent communication passing between them. "Alright. How about we make a deal?"

"What are you offering?"

More communication passes between them. "Try to score a goal against me. I'll give you three shots to score, but if you miss, you four have to de-fork our field. Today. Before our game.

"And if I score?"

He shrugs. "You get a free pass and we're stuck here cleaning up the mess."

I glance at Jameia and an idea springs to mind. "Not good enough. I didn't fork your field, your friend there can vouch for me."

She bites her lip, the sight alone making my dick twitch.

"Okay. So if you score, what do you want?" she asks, joining the conversation.

I consider my options and decide I've got nothing to lose. "A kiss," I tell her.

Her mouth parts and everyone around us makes *ooooOOOH* sounds, getting riled up as they wait to see how she answers. She's going to say no. I can see it in her eyes and for whatever reason, I don't want her to. She's hot as hell and while I've got my eyes on Kasey, something tells me Jameia would be a fun interlude.

"But if you're afraid to risk it, I get it. It's not like your boys here stand a chance."

She snorts. "You're that confident you can score against Gabe?"

I look from him to the field. I mean, I've never played soccer before, but how hard can it be? All I've got to do is kick the ball in the giant ass goal. It's not like he can cover the whole thing.

"Yeah. I guess I am."

"Come on, Meme. You know I've got this," Gabe encourages.

She looks at him, her expression pinched before she gives a single nod. "I'm only agreeing because he's not a student. You know my rules."

"Yeah, yeah. No fucking the freshies."

"Oh, so it's fucking we're putting on the table here?"

"Definitely not," she snaps, but I don't miss the heat in her gaze.

I lick my lips. "No worries. I'll settle for the kiss."

The boys lead the way to the field and Gabe grabs a ball and a pair of gloves from the gym bag he abandoned near the gate.

"You need any instructions?" he asks.

"I just have to kick it in the net, right?"

He nods. "It's a little more complicated than that, but yeah. We'll treat it like a penalty kick. You'll start here." He leads me to a line in the field and sets the ball down. "This is twelve yards from the goal line. You have to kick from here. You can't rush me to score, got it."

I nod. "Got it."

He smirks, an arrogant swagger in his step as he positions himself in front of the goal. "Whenever you're ready, man."

I take a deep breath, focus in on that place inside myself where all I see is the ball and the end zone. This isn't football, but the feeling is similar. The goal. The drive to score.

The girls offer encouragement from the sidelines, but for the most part, I tune it out. Taking a deep breath, I take a few steps back, giving myself some room to work with, and line myself up with the goal. I don't want to come at it straight on. He's expecting that. I don't play this sport but I'm sure there's more skill to it than I'm giving it credit. I take in the width of the goal and decide to aim for the top right corner. That will force him to lunge to his left and I have a feeling he's right-handed and is stronger going that direction.

Inhaling deep, I zero in on the ball, bounce on my heels a few times and jog to close the small distance, pushing off and bringing my leg back before I swing forward. I power through the kick, following it all the way through. The ball sails through the air, arrowing right where I intended, in the top right corner at rapid speed. Gabe's eyes widen a second before he lunges for the ball, but that split second of surprise costs him and he misses, his fingers not ever grazing the leather before it collides with the net.

Allie and Kasey are screaming, Bibiana bouncing up and down. A smile breaks out over my face and I meet Jameia's stunned expression. Without hesitating, I head straight for her, my steps confident. She looks to her left and right, as if expecting someone to swoop in and save her. Sorry, pretty girl, not today.

When she's a foot away, I reach out, pull her towards me with one hand on the small of her back, the other cupping the side of her neck, and I press my lips against hers. Hoots and hollers go up around us and she holds herself rigid in my arms.

That's not going to work.

Pressing firmer against her, I nip at her bottom lip and she gasps, giving me the opening I need to sweep my tongue into her mouth. I stroke my tongue over hers and it only takes a few seconds before she's kissing me back, fingers curling into the fabric of my shirt. Sparks of sensation race through my body and I groan against her lips. My dick hardens in my pants and I'm sure she can feel it, but it doesn't look like she minds. Thank fuck for that.

Her tongue darts out and swipes across my lip and I tilt her head, deepening the kiss. Reality must catch up to her though, because the next thing I know, she's biting my lip, hard, and I rear back to glare at her.

"You got your prize," she says, voice breathless.

I lick over my abused lip, tasting blood, and smile at her. "Yeah. I guess I did."

She steps away and the next thing I know I'm being tackled by Allies friends and we tumble to the ground. "Bro! That was sick. Please tell me Allie was not full of shit when she said you were looking at making a change and yeah, I get it. She meant football, not fútbol but seriously, man. Think about it. We could use someone like you on the team."

I untangle myself from the dog pile and climb up to my feet. "I hate to break it to you but uh, she lied."

Julio shoots her a glare, and she ducks behind Bibiana. "Alight, alright. So that wasn't the plan, but you'll consider it, yeah?"

I shake my head. "I don't know. I mean, I've never played. That was one kick— "

"I know talent when I see it and you've got it. You can score ,and if you already play ball then I'll assume you can work under pressure?"

I nod.

"Great. Next weekend, come back and we'll have you try out in front of Coach. Just tell me you'll think about?"

I press my lips together and shake my head.

"We need a new striker and we've got a full ride scholarship on the table for the right one."

My ears perk up. "Full ride?"

He meets Jameia's gaze. "Wanna give him the deets?"

I frown. Why would he ask her to fill me in? She isn't on the team. She visibly swallows and sweeps the curls out of her face. "Yeah. So if you have what it takes and we invite you to play, you'll have tuition, dorm, and a food credit provided."

Fuck. That's not a bad deal. But I love football. I'm not sure I want to leave the game. Though a full ride means I'm not relying on my parents to help me out with tuition. It's a lot to consider.

"You said we. How do you factor into all this?"

Julio slaps me on the back before hooking his arm over my shoulder. "Meme here is our assistant coach."

My eyes widen at that. So that's why she said she doesn't date students. It all makes perfect sense. My eyes land on her mouth and she touches her lips, thinking about the kiss we just shared. Maybe coming to play at PacNorth isn't a bad idea after all.

Want more? Check out The Savage to see more from the boys at PacNorth and Cruel Promise to learn what's next in store for Dom & Kasey

What to Read Next

**Dominique & Kasey's Story continues in
Cruel Promise**

Grief is a fickle bi*ch, and I'll do anything to escape her.
That includes sleeping with my brother's very off-limits best
friend.

Dominique Price wants me.
My body. My mind. My soul.
And he can have me.
Behind closed doors and away from prying eyes.
As long as helps me forget my pain, and promises to stay the
hell away from my heart, I'll be his.
And for a short while, he'll be mine.

But, we're playing a dangerous game. One whose rules are
swiftly being ignored.
I want him. Need him. Might even be addicted to him.

Only, happily ever after was never in the cards for us.
And it looks like I'm the idiot who forgot that.

Go to https://amzn.to/3c3hN5j
to order your copy of Cruel Promise.

A Note from the Author

I know what you're thinking. Where is the rest of Dominique & Kasey's story? Why can't you have all of it right now? To be honest, I didn't know there would be two books for this couple until I was nearly finished with Cruel Devil. Things just sort of worked out this way. Dominique and Kasey have so much to work through and I didn't want to rush their relationship. Once you read Cruel Promise, I think you'll agree I made the right call.

Special thanks to Lisa and Cynthia for helping me push through this book and coming in at the final hour to help me polish it and make Cruel Devil shine. I couldn't have done this without you. Thank you to Jacqueline and Bridgett for the last minute read throughs and to Christina and Nicole for all of the help in my crazy author world while I hid in my writer cave to get this book done.

Thank you to all of my awesome readers for your patience while I wrote this book. We had some delays and some injuries and it's been a rollercoaster but I appreciate you sticking around for the ride.

And a special thanks to the girls in the sprint room. You know who you are. Thank you for being there for all those late night sprints and for not scolding me when I was still going as you eastern timers were just waking up.

On a personal note, I would be incredibly grateful if you took a moment to leave an honest review for the book when you are done reading.

xoxo

Daniela Romero

About the Author

Daniela Romero is a USA Today and Wall Street Journal bestselling author. She enjoys writing steamy, new-adult and paranormal romance that delivers an emotional roller coaster sure to take your breath away.

Her books feature a diverse cast of characters with rich and vibrant cultures in an effort to effectively portray the world we all live in. One that is so beautifully colorful.

Daniela is a Bay Area native though she currently lives in Washington State with her sarcastic husband and their three tiny terrors.

In her free time, Daniela enjoys frequent naps, binge reading her favorite romance books, and is known to crochet while watching television because her ADHD brain can never do just one thing at a time.

Stop by her website to find all the fun and unique ways you can stalk her. And while you're there you can check out some free bonus scenes from your favorite books, learn about her Patreon, order signed copies of her books, and swoon over her gorgeous alternative cover editions.

www.daniela-romero.com
You can join my newsletter by visiting
https://hi.switchy.io/VIP

Made in the USA
Monee, IL
27 July 2023

39901374R00180